THE HAUNTING OF WALTER

RABINOWITZ

by
Judie Rae

Kali, be with us.
Violence, destruction, receive our homage.
Help us to bring darkness into the light,
To lift out the pain, the anger,
Where it can be seen for what it is—
The balance-wheel for our vulnerable, aching love
Put the wild hunger where it belongs,
Within the act of creation,
Crude power that forges a balance
Between hate and love.

Help us to be the always hopeful
Gardeners of the spirit
Who know that without darkness
Nothing comes to birth
As without light
Nothing flowers.

May Sarton

THE HAUNTING OF WALTER RABINOWITZ

by
Judie Rae

Artemis Books
Penn Valley, California
2019

First edition published 2019 by Artemis Books
Trade Distribution by Independent Publishers Group

ISBN: 978-1-945765-09-4   (trade paperback)
978-1-945765-10-0   (EPUB format)
978-1-945765-11-7   (Mobipocket format)
978-1-945765-12-4   (PDF format)

Cover design by Gailyn Porter
Artemis Books Editor: Iven Lourie

Parts of Chapter 8 of this novel in earlier forms appeared in *Kaleidoscope Magazine* and on line at *Women's Voices for Change.*

Published by Artemis Books
PO Box 1108
Penn Valley, CA 95946
USA

Phone: (800) 869-0658 or (530) 277-5380
E-mail: artemisbooks@gmail.com
Website: http://www.artemis-books.com

:

DEDICATION

This book is dedicated to my sisters everywhere, as well as to my daughters and granddaughters, especially Hannah, who showed me what true courage is.

And to Will: steadfast partner, steadfast friend.

ACKNOWLEDGMENTS

Many thanks are due to dear friends, all writers and artists, who supported me unconditionally, and saw this novel through process to completion. Among those to whom I owe a debt of gratitude are Gene Berson, Judy Brackett Crowe, Betsy Graziani Fasbinder, Molly Fisk, Iven Lourie, Gailyn Porter, and Julie Valin.

Chapter One

1988

Effie Latimer left in the fall, which was lousy timing any way you looked at it: There were the holidays to consider and her sentimental attachment to ritual. But beyond that, for a college instructor of English who had some appreciation for the symbolic nature of the seasons, who understood archetypal criticism, who understood there was a proper time for leave-takings, the act was particularly unforgivable. Spring was the season of new beginnings. But then Effie had always had a lousy sense of timing. Before her marriage, there had once been a man in her life who said to her, "Of course I love you but the timing is wrong. Come back in twenty years and we'll read poetry together by the fire. You'll be Marianne Moore and I'll be…" She couldn't remember what poet of note he had chosen; he had so many favorites. He told her she reminded him of Sylvia Plath. Effie was quite certain he was referring to her intensity, to her painful poems, but perhaps in the end he was giving her some sort of oblique hint. She might have considered obliging if just one person would have appreciated the guilt she bestowed. So much for emulating suicidal poets. Now, years later, during a separation from her husband, James, she entertained the notion of looking him up, but then, what for? Marianne Moore was all right, but not the sort of reading that sustained. She might have considered someone along the lines of Charles Bukowski, but that picture of him in the *LA Times* with his beautiful wife, who was at least twenty years younger, made her mad as hell. The old goat.

The fall, November particularly, was a problem. In the past she had gone all out for Thanksgiving, preparing a feast for fifty. Now, she could no more put fifty people in the trailer she had rented than she could fly.

"You are geographically inaccessible," Nicholas, a writer friend, informed her. "Who's going to find you in this godforsaken place? You want to get laid, move down to the coast." *Getting laid* was not a priority on Effie's list although she did entertain some guilt regarding her friends wandering the hills for days in search of a holiday meal. At the last minute she was rescued from this trauma of indecision by an old acquaintance with a self-basting turkey to share. Effie brought dessert. The pain of separation from her family was assuaged somewhat by Uncle Meyer who carved the bird while singing "When Irish Eyes Are Smiling," a song that made Effie cry so he switched to "Bloody Mary Is the Girl I Love." Why Uncle Meyer, who was notably Jewish, chose to sing about bright-eyed colleens was not entirely clear to her until Aunt Rose explained: "He thinks it's the only song that does justice to his voice."

And what was James doing? Calling her, that's what he was doing. Asking her how to make her famous chestnut stuffing. It would not have been in her best interest to refuse him the recipe, so she complied, deleting only two ingredients: the apples and the wild rice. Some things are sacrosanct and she had no intention of sharing her secret with a horde of James' newfound friends. He got the house and the girls, who elected to stay with the comforts of their own bedrooms and commute to college; she maintained the integrity of her chestnut dressing.

Many of their friends felt sorry for James and didn't mind telling her so. "He's so skinny, Effie. The poor man is suffering. You should see him in the kitchen. It's pathetic the way he tries so hard." Which was just like James, winning the affection of all their friends by acting the nebbish, a Woody Allen who used the blender and forgot to put on the lid. So what if the ceiling was covered with piña coladas and guacamole. She wasn't budging.

No one felt sorry for *her*. No one saw James' passive-aggressive behavior. Nicholas had this to say: "You've chosen to live up there like the princess on the glass mountain, Effie, like the buzzard waiting to lure unsuspecting victims into your lair."

"I'm not trying to lure anyone into my lair, Nicholas. And buzzards, for your information, don't lure. They survive on carrion."

"Exactly. Dead things. By the time any man makes his way to you he *is* half dead." The mountains Nick referred to were the Santa Monica's, a range that ran through the belly of Los Angeles and down to the sea. Many of the canyons that traversed the hills were home to eccentric, nature-loving folk like Effie, who, for the most part, preferred the company of coyotes to lounge lizards. Nicholas, who understood her fondness for writers, continued, "Name two writers who are also mountain climbers."

"Sir Edmund Hillary and Peter Matthiessen."

"Name three."

"I like it up here, Nick. It's quiet. I see deer and bobcat and roadrunners."

"And rattlesnakes and scorpions and poison oak."

"Into every life a little acid rain must fall."

"Effie, go back to James. He loves you."

"Funny kind of love. He smothers me. Right now he's having the time of his life creating dependencies for the girls, avoiding figuring out what he's going to do with himself because they *need* him. And when they're done needing him, maybe he'll get lucky and we'll have grandkids. Plus, I can't handle the passive-aggressiveness."

"Examples?" Nick asked.

"I can give you plenty. Recall when I had the op-ed article in the *LA Times*? For years, James has had a habit of walking to get the newspaper on the weekends. But the day the article appeared, he was on the roof. Instead of celebrating with me, he said, 'I thought you wanted me to clean the gutters. Today seemed like a good morning to get the leaves out.' I wanted to celebrate having an article in the paper, but he was upset about who knows what. Remember a few years ago when I got my master's? I went through the ceremony because I wanted to impress upon the kids the importance of an education. James took photos. Immediately after the ceremony he departed on a business trip. When he got back, he told me he had lost the film."

Nick sighed.

"No one thanks you for the sacrifices made on their behalf, Nicholas. I'm tired of buying into that." Nick shook his head. "I love James. You know that. I just don't think I can live with him. We want different things. We always have. He reads *Forbes*. I read *Mother Earth News*. I want simplicity. He wants to make money. It's how he defines himself. I suggested we move out of the smog, out of the city, Oregon maybe. 'And what would we do there?' he responded. 'It's not money,' I told him. 'It's imagination.' 'Fine,' he said. 'When the money runs out we can all sit down to dinner and *imagine* we're eating.'

'I could teach,' I told him. 'That's great,' he said. 'I can't.'"

"And what of the other one?"

Nick noticed Effie's pixie face turn grim. She shook her dark curls. Tears glistened in her large grey eyes. "Walter Rabinowitz is a terrific writer, Nick. But he's a lousy mountain climber."

When Effie first walked up the stairs of the university and into the second-story classroom, into the creative writing seminar, she had no idea her life was about to change. She wanted to pursue a second master's, share her love of writing with those equally smitten by the printed word. If she had been as intuitive as she claimed to be, if her witch's powers had been running full bore, she might have suspected something was afoot the moment she and Walter Rabinowitz locked eyes. Certainly she felt no immediate physical response to the man, who looked to be in his fifties; he was tall, lanky, balding and half hidden behind thick-framed glasses. Effie thought he looked like Arthur Miller. No, the response was far worse than physical. "We don't get to choose to whom we're attracted, but we do have the power to choose whether or not we become involved with someone," Julie, her therapist, had said to her some time after the fact. By that Effie assumed that Julie was asking her if she thought the process was a rational one. Was Julie suggesting her unspoken neurotic needs were swirling around Walter's neurotic needs, playing games with them, bonding? The unconscious melding with the unconscious? She'd have to ask Julie. If so, Effie thought it terribly unfair that she had little say in the matter.

Initially, she didn't even like the man, who struck her as brilliant, loud, and cocky. He had a habit of pounding on the table to make his point, a trick that repeatedly caused her to jump out of her shoes. And yet, she recognized in him the same absurdist, iconoclastic worldview, which in itself was rare.

And he was funny.

And he liked her writing.

Again, after the fact, he told her he liked her body, so there too she doubted it was a purist's response to her work. But initially he said he liked her writing and kept his mouth shut about the packaging. Which was just as well, for if she had even suspected a sexual attraction on his part she would have hauled off and whapped him one. Now she wished she had done so, just for good measure.

It had been Effie and not Walter who first sent out "feelers," a matter which subsequently caused her a great deal of remorse until Julie explained that Effie had merely responded to what was there in the first place. Julie was terrific for alleviating guilt. All along Walter had been forwarding unconscious, sexual messages and she had bought into that, misinterpreting his friendliness as an equivalent desire to share with her a love of books as well as his superior knowledge of the writing process.

The afternoon she decided she loved him they sat together in the university cafeteria discussing her novel in progress. "You have a gift," he told her. "And a unique way of looking at things."

She smiled at him. "I've discovered you can't make

others join you there." She hoped the sadness she felt was hidden from this man.

"No," he answered. "It's lonely. Music helps." The look that passed between them was loaded with meaning and intensity. Effie, had she been wise, would have chosen that precise moment to run like hell, to scurry away from the subtle, subdued advances of the writer/professor.

They bantered. Walter employed words such as *oxymoron* to describe the quirky, contradictory, rhetorical imagery used by the local poet bards. And, she suspected, to show off. "I thought an oxymoron was a dumb Brit," she responded.

She told him of the problems she was having with her local gas station, with the attendant who was running credit card scams. "Do you know anyone who breaks kneecaps for a living?"

"I used to," Walter answered, "but then he became a vegetarian."

He told her he was divorcing. "It's not acrimonious," he said. It certainly wasn't. It was so un-acrimonious that he and his wife continued to live together. He told her of an affair he had with a student. Later she remarked to her therapist, "How many vulnerable women are there in the entire county of Los Angeles? This man seems pretty astute at finding us." Or they found him. She was no longer sure how the process functioned, but she was working up a genuine distrust of her antennae's honing abilities.

For months the intimacies they shared arrived by mail. Effie felt herself drawn to the magic of Walter's words and ultimately to the man himself. She delighted in reading between the lines, in composing missives that she suspected caused him to do the same. And, after all, he was her mentor, there to help her through the mysterious process of fiction writing.

Did she feel guilty for this emotional flirtation? James was gone so much, so engaged with his career, so emotionally unavailable to her that it was not difficult to rationalize her behavior, although later she would come to see that she had acted in hurtful, immoral ways. Her friend, Ramona, had suggested Effie have an affair if she had to, and keep her mouth shut, thus preserving her marriage and home. Instead Effie told James about Walter and moved out.

So Rabinowitz became her mentor. Effie, who had had some success as a writer of children's books, professed to him a desire to create stories of substance.Walter's passion for Gerard Manley Hopkins as well as the poets of the metaphysical school was yet another connection. Effie liked Hopkins as well, but that John Donne stuff left her particularly untouched. Only much later was she able to figure out Walter's attachment; it was much easier to intercourse with the powers that be, guilt free, when one's understanding included a firm awareness that the earlier bards had gotten away with it. Effie pictured Walter arguing with God—and almost winning—railing against the unjust circumstances that kept a man of his infinite grace, style, talent, and intellectual abilities mired in the muck. Did she say charm? Also, most certainly, a man of his charm. Walter had years ago written a six-hundred-page novel loosely based on the life and times of Andrew Marvell, which to date had been rejected by twenty-seven publishers. A wiser Effie would have taken another look at the poem "To His Coy Mistress." Instead, she commiserated with him, dreamed privately of comforting the man, of holding his shaggy head to her breast. Walter must have shared her dreams for while they talked of story structure, of character development, of point of view, she caught him gazing discreetly down her blouse. He responded by congratulating her on her considerable writing talents, explaining how in time they would coalesce into something grand. Of course she believed him.

The lesson to be learned from all this to date, he wrote to her, *is that what is written, be it entirely a fabrication, a bald-faced lie, an ornamentation, or an accounting of an event, carries with it the passions, humors, and fantasies of the writer. If the effect is blandness, do not question the writing;*

examine the writer. The next thing to throw away, after the
adverb, is the conscience, or the pangs of remorse. The only
things allowable in that context are, oh, if I had only felt it
more intensely, and oh, if I had only written it better. From
that point forward, Effie discarded her conscience as she
would have discarded an old dust rag. When the guru spoke,
she listened. (That this was an issue of her own self-esteem,
did not cross her mind until much later.)

In addition to access to information on the writing life,
Effie sought self-knowledge and independence. Here, too,
Walter seemed to have some a priori grasp of the process. And
so with little verbalization they acknowledged the chemistry
between them, agreed to become tour guides for each other in
terrain that appeared on no map, for exhibitions found in no
art gallery.

In the interim Effie explained to her college classes
about archetypes in literature, put them in touch with the
collective unconscious, told them to be aware of how the
mythic quest was manipulated by filmmakers. Privately she
wondered why all the prototypes: Luke Skywalker, King
Arthur, Odysseus, were male. The discrepancy bothered her.
She searched for female characters who fit the stereotype: a
personification of a culture's mythology, an explorer, a
philosopher, an adventurer of the mind, a woman with a vision
quest who transformed the world. A woman who responded to
the call to adventure. A woman who became the dragon slayer
and who was challenged to follow the wisdom of her heart.

Joan of Arc fit the ideal, with one grand exception: a
Joanie roast struck Effie as a less than fitting ending. Some
metaphor. The bright light was Walter, her mentor, her
mythmaker. What Effie was to discover was that each of us
must make our own myths.

And hope to hell they last.

ᔕᕦ ᔕᕦ ᔕᕦ

It was not your initial intent to intrude. You liked looking at yourself
third person. You liked the distance between you. What happened

to change your mind was this: you and Effie tromped off to a week-long writing seminar in San Francisco where you met a well-dressed woman writer whose criticism you admired, who said to you, "The problem with your character is that she is a hateful bitch." Disbelieving, you blinked back tears and ran and hid in the corner where you seriously considered: 1. killing yourself; 2. killing the well-dressed woman writer; 3. killing Effie.

You did none of the above because you've discovered that some time and distance—you gave yourself ten minutes—are helpful in putting matters back into perspective. So were the comments of the man who came up to you after the seminar and said, "Sounds as though you just received the famous blankety-blank put down." (Filling in her name would be tacky.)

"Perhaps she's right," you said, entertaining notions of rowing to the Bermuda Triangle.

"Look," he told you, "you are representative of a certain glamorous Southern California lifestyle that many Marin County matrons find offensive."

What lifestyle? You didn't feel particularly glamorous in your jeans and old baggy sweater. (All right, they were *tight* jeans.) And she had called you *cutie*. "Do you really think that's it?" Effie said to the seminar participant. You wanted to believe the man but your relationship with Walter has left you sadly suspicious of male motives.

"Yes, I do. Your writing is wonderfully bitchy, but your character is not."

"Perhaps I should try first person."

"Ignore her."

"But she just told me my writing stinks, my mother wears jockey shorts, and I don't belong on the face of the earth. I think I need a few minutes to absorb this."

He laughed.

"I thought the definition of a good story had something to do with an interesting character attempting to overcome ostensibly insurmountable odds in order to achieve a worthwhile goal. The key word is *interesting*, not likable. Perhaps it's my unreliable narrator?"

You can hear Walter now telling you that this author

intrusion is too clever. You're not trying to be clever; you're trying to be honest. You're trying to understand. Walter was always telling you how too clever creates difficulty and in that matter he was correct. You recognize that women who assert themselves are in danger of offending entire segments of the population. It's rather no-win.

Is Effie Latimer one confused woman? Read on.

Chapter Two

"Promise me that you'll see me through this. You have to act as my support group, like AA or Overeaters Anonymous. Every time I feel the urge to phone him, I call you instead. Agreed?"

"Of course we agree, Effie. You know that. Blythe, please hand me a croissant." Lucy smiled at Effie and took a hefty bite from the roll. Effie's writing group met twice a month to read, to critique, to psychoanalyze, to commiserate. Effie found solace in the fact they were all behind her one hundred percent, except for Lucy, who was behind her but who considered her nuts.

Effie challenged them all. "Even if it's three in the morning?"

Lucy's eyes widened. "Three in the morning? You're not really going to want to call him at three in the morning, are you?" She chewed thoughtfully on her croissant.

"Lucy!" Ramona glared at her. "Effie, we will be there for you day or night. Thick or thin. Right, girls?" Effie knew Ramona meant no denigration of women when she used the term *girls*. Ramona was fond of saying, "Any woman worth her salt is part child."

Blythe looked skeptical. "Right. But I'm going to have to move the phone to my side of the bed. Arnold would have a fit if you woke him up at three."

"Oh, to hell with Arnold!" Ramona raged. "Don't call Blythe at three, Effie. Call me."

"I was just explaining how it is with me, Ramona. That's all. I can handle Arnold, Effie. If you need to call, call."

Lucy looked around the trailer. "You've really fixed this place up, Effie. It's cute. Really cute."

"The couch makes into a bed for when the girls come over."

"I'm jealous," Blythe admitted. "To be able to live like this—simply." Blythe admired Effie's groupings of fresh flowers.

"It's all illusion, Blythe. Believe me. And it is *not* simple. Thoreau must have known something I don't."

"Yeah," Ramona interrupted, "like the fact his mother would wash his dirty clothes when he walked them home."

Effie snickered, then continued. "I've tried being in touch with my solitude. Mostly I end up in tears. I've tried to commune with nature. The mouse in the cupboard and I have come to an understanding. It doesn't make its appearance when I have guests, and I leave it alone."

"You have a mouse in here?" Lucy asked. She shuddered.

"Let's hope that mouse is separated from her husband and *he* got the kids." Ramona moved from the wicker settee to the floor.

Lucy squealed. "I think I felt the baby move!" The other three women stared at Lucy's abdomen in rapt attention. A sense of wonder permeated the room. Lucy smiled beatifically.

"You are going to make a terrific mother," Effie told Lucy. All nodded in agreement. "Let's go over our stories now, shall we?"

The writing group's practice was to give their manuscripts to each other for reading at home. "Why do we do this?" Lucy asked.

"It saves time," Ramona answered. "Plus, it gives us all opportunity to make comments in the margins."

"I'm not sure I like it," Lucy said.

"The rest of us do, don't we ladies?" Ramona looked at Blythe and Effie, who both nodded in the affirmative. "All right then, let's get started. Shall we talk about Effie's story first? We worked with her story last at our last meeting."

"Okay," Effie agreed. "This is something I've been working on for some time."

The women studied her story.

Taking Flight

Dust in a shaft of sunlight. Fragmented, she stops to watch the particles curl and duck, coloring the air. Cerulean sparks drift, enveloped by a larger sense of fancy, as necessity and obligations wrap around her. Time to acknowledge her own blue fire: dust in space.

She lifts the books from the nightstand to wipe away the gathered molecules of grime. She stares at the reading material, a computer programmer's reference, a Wall Street Journal, *the paperback* Blue Highways *she pressed on him. Unread.*

Against the far wall, an antique stand. Tumbling forth from the shelves, abundant, overflowing, her books. Her journal, her many notebooks, the works that sustain and nourish her.

Two strangers inhabit this room. She can feel the poetry fighting against the concepts and confines of time, the technology, the predictable, the regular. The tools of his livelihood repressing feeling, undermining passion. And she, the parasite of that livelihood.

She has made up her mind. For months now, she has lived with the notion, the image of herself alone. In daydreams she seeks a place to meditate, to write, a place above the sea, a mountaintop, a place to test her gifts, a place to cultivate her own resources.

The calling voice will not be silenced. She desires to be aligned with her passion, to accede to it, not to fight, to deny or subvert her instincts. She wants to be vulnerable. Intuition tells her she will be able to absorb her own pain, though she is in danger of being consumed by the pain of others.

Uncertainties, ambivalence, march through her head. The disenchantments grow. If she stays, there is the problem of her becoming mean in spirit. Already alienated, she survives by transporting herself to other places, a gift she discovered in childhood.

She had wanted to give them so much of herself, only to be rebuked, misunderstood, unheard. One Indian summer night, years ago, her husband out of town, she had wakened her son to watch with her a meteor shower. The boy, an inaccessible twelve-year-old, had lain beside her on the hard redwood picnic table and stared dully into the night sky. When he threatened to fall asleep, unimpressed by what the heavens had to offer, she had prodded him. She knew his memories were not of the sky raining fire, but rather of her constant goading, poking him into consciousness. She was always foisting miracles onto others, which for them never materialized. She realized, finally, that the union with one's own possibilities cannot be forced. Her desires complicated love.

When was it, exactly, that she had begun to view her current situation as a trap? She could not pinpoint one day in time, one moment, when the feeling came. The revelation had been muzzy, nebulous at first, and then the blinding clarity.

Her children, she acknowledged, both broadened and enriched her life, and she loved them so, yet she knew that the productions of herself that would continue to satisfy came not only from her womb, but from her soul. Would other women admit such?

The trap is cushioned, steel teeth cleverly disguised, wrapped not in down, but in duty, exigencies. And yet she knows that everything she desires has to come from inside. All else seems excess.

But oh, what guilt! Women, hips cast wide, designed to carry babies as well as the burdens of the ages. Already she can see in the outline of her daughters' thin figures the ability to lug through time not only the love products of their future unions, but the encumbrances, which she now is just beginning to understand. Were there words to warn them? But youth never listen. The message, she knew, would be misconstrued. I speak to spare you, daughters of my loins, daughters of the earth. Spare them what? In our choice of lovers, friends, teachers, those who rearrange our lives, we are guided by forces we seldom understand. Accidental? She is beginning to think not. So what is left to say? Discover your own strength.

Yes, this surely. The capacity to wound is carried on from generation to generation. Perhaps on the tip of a chromosome rests the hurting gene, invisible to scientists but recognized by all humanity. Hide your wounds inside where they do not show and they find a way forward, the capacity to injure transmitted from parent to child. What is left to say? Only this: Take your life into your own fine hands.

From her womb had come three treasures. The lullabies she sang to them, she sang to herself, slowly dulling her natural courage until confinement became almost comfortable. A song drowns out rage. A caged bird sings.

She blames no one but herself, her mouth fixed in determination. And yet there remains a capacity for joy, from the other world she frequents. So many excuses exist to feel only pain, excuses not to live, not to see the wonder in a night sky, even a sky devoid of meteors. She will not cross that barrier into bleakness. She hopes that nothing she does is without meaning, nothing that she endures does not contain a seed of creation. Perhaps she has internalized too much; what she seeks now is form.

In her head a poem begins. Words dance before her eyes. Her entire being—flesh, spirit, mind—join in a union, concentrate on a single shaft of sunlight. Daily frustrations fall away and she becomes an instrument of experience. She feels weightless, strong, the blue fire no longer dust in space but a naked soul in balance. Centered. Embosomed in a state of grace.

"Well, what do you think?" Effie waited for her friends to respond.

"Oh, Effie, you are so forty." Ramona's wonderful face lit up with amusement.

"Forty-six, actually." Effie felt herself grow testy, defensive. She looked at Ramona, who sat on her left. Ramona's long, paisley skirt caught the sunlight through the window. To Effie, Ramona was a bright, shining spark.

"Ramona is probably at least half-right, Effie. Haven't you read *Passages?*" Blythe offered up as proof a book title at least once every meeting. "Gail Sheehy says…"

"I don't care what she says!"

"Effie!" Lucy intoned. "Take it easy. Blythe was just trying to help. We love you."

"I know." She choked back the emotion of the moment. "I love you too. It's just that…"

"Your response is natural under the circumstances. Sheehy says…"

"Blythe." Ramona's thick eyebrows raised in warning.

Effie tried to explain to her writing group the heroine's journey. "The story has to open with the heroine appearing restless. Something is missing from her life. There is a feeling of destiny."

"The conflict is not overt enough," Lucy said. Lucy, Ramona's niece, was only twenty-six.

"Bullshit," said Ramona, who never said *bullshit*, but who, Effie knew, understood her conflict, understood about Walter, and who once had developed a nice little crush of her own on a solitary artist/teacher who shared his ideas on art with her. "The story reeks of conflict, Effie. I think it's wonderful."

"Thank you."

"I don't see it," Lucy said. "There's not enough action to sustain all the internalization."

"It's an *internal* story." Effie loved it when Ramona, whose criticism she admired, rushed to her defense.

"What do you think, Blythe?" Effie watched Blythe deliberate. Blythe was usually cautious in her choice of words. She played for a moment with the crumbs on her plate. "Well. Your story worries me because I see the heroine on the edge psychologically. Over a period of time that could be disruptive."

"We are not talking psychology, Blythe. We are talking writing. Criticize the *writing*." Ramona's look dared her to do otherwise.

"But all of Effie's stories, her poems as of late, are saying the same thing. I'm very worried about you, Effie."

"I'm fine." She looked at all of them. "Really."

"And you will be fine as long as you keep writing." Ramona smiled at her, instilling a few meager grains of confidence.

Blythe, miffed, retorted. "She can't write all the time. She has to live in the real world."

"So how do you handle the conflict?" Effie knew she need not elaborate on the struggle.

"I compartmentalize," offered Lucy. "I just wish I had a larger compartment for writing."

"Ladies, we are looking at the kind of woman who can successfully handle an affair." Ramona chuckled.

"Why do you say that?" Lucy looked offended.

"Everything nice and neat. Nothing crossing over, getting messy and confusing. I believe a lot of men think this way." Effie knew just what Ramona meant and she envied Lucy's capacity to divvy up her life. Lucky, lucky Lucy.

Blythe spoke. "You haven't been married long enough, Lucy. Or writing long enough. Or trying to do both. Sooner or later the resentment will get to you. The anger will come."

Lucy, near tears, looked at them all. "I think you people are awful."

"No, we're not," Ramona said. "We're just being honest. And when you start writing more about yourself, things that get to the heart of the matter, you'll realize that."

Blythe spoke. "If I couldn't do what Lucy does, separate things, I'd go crazy too." She looked at each of them in turn. "A trip to the market, if I didn't know the other was waiting, would do me in."

"I envy you." Effie swallowed hard. "I can't do that."

"So how do you manage?" Lucy asked.

"I try to make a poem out of it. I get into the feel of things: the sights, the sounds. Sometimes, though, I run into trouble, sensory overload and all that." Effie did not tell them that this over-attention to stimuli, to what she called sensory shrapnel, scared the hell out of her. She thought perhaps it was one of the reasons she was always getting lost. She homed in on the hum of the car, or the feel of the sun on her arm, or the smells after a rain, and pretty soon she had no idea where she was, or worse, where she was supposed to be. Sometimes she wondered if she was going crazy. Maybe Blythe was right: She was on the edge.

"The issue of control is an interesting one," Ramona remarked. "We all live with the illusion of it, and in some sense daily life perpetuates that belief, but really…"

"But really what?" Blythe asked. "Of course we're in control. Can I pour us all more coffee, Effie?"

Effie smiled, noting how Blythe fooled even herself. "I wonder what it would take, Blythe," Ramona said, "to blow the myth of your power to control sky high?"

Lucy interrupted. "Let's get back to the writing, shall we? I would like your feedback on my latest chapter."

The group agreed and handed Effie back her manuscript. "I made a few comments in the margins," Blythe said.

"I did too," Lucy said.

"Thank you," Effie responded. "All of you. I don't know what I'd do without you in my life."

♣♣♣♣

Ramona stayed to talk with Effie after the others had left. "I'm so lonely, Ramona. I think I could die from the pain of this."

Ramona smiled sadly. "But you won't, dear heart. It only feels that way."

"I feel like such a fool. I've hurt my family, my kids…"

"Yes, well, most people only move out in their heads. You had to go for the whole shot. Most people stay at home and have their little affairs, that way keeping family, friends, flowers, house, etc., all intact." Ramona inspected the trailer.

"Isn't there some legal something about giving up rights when you move out?"

"Probably. I don't much care, except for my children. And James is letting my flowers die."

"And what about what's his name...the writer?"

"Walter. Haven't heard from him, which is a big part of my sadness."

" He's scared, Effie. You terrified him."

"How?"

"By being the way you are: confrontational, honest, able to make decisions."

"But he said he'd be here."

"Right. That was when you were moving out in your head. Or his head. When it was safe. Now you've forced him to deal with the real issues."

"Hell."

"Yes, that too."

"He's a hell of a writer."

"Ah, yet. They're the worst. Able to delude themselves with their own words. If they're terribly clever, they never even suspect."

"How come you know so much?"

"I told you. Because it happened to me. The artist I shared the office with for two semesters. The whole time he alluded to the fact he was separated from his wife. I believed him primarily because *he* believed him. I found out later that it wasn't true."

Effie sighed. "He moved out in his head?"

"Exactly."

"God."

"Exactly."

"Then to hell with him. To hell with them all. The thing that so disturbs me about him, Ramona, is that it means my antennae, my intuition, is all wrong. I hate that."

"Wait a minute. Your antennae were up and flourishing, right on target for him as a writer, as a mentor. There you didn't go wrong."

Effie thought about this.

Ramona continued, "Sounds as though you didn't use that intuition to understand him as a person, and when you did, it was too late."

"I never thought of it that way."

"Intuition doesn't always work, when you're too emotionally involved to see straight, for example. I still say he's afraid."

"Of what?"

"Who can say? He probably doesn't know. Maybe he doesn't want to feel guilty or responsible for his role in you leaving your family."

"He had no responsibility."

Ramona engaged in her famous eyebrow raise. "Didn't he?"

"Why are relationships so often a process of building walls against each other?"

"Because most of us would rather idealize than see what is. We want to escape to some romantic future rather than accept what is in the present."

How could Effie hold that against him? She too clung to her own limitations. He was, after all, only a man. "How come you're so smart, Ramona?"

"I don't try to be smart, friend. I just try to be kind. I just try to do my best, whatever that is. I try to do my best with kindness."

Effie awakened from a dream, confused. The images pounded in her head. A cold sweat drenched her. Effie, in her night vision, was six weeks pregnant. Her stomach was knotted, tight. She was losing the baby. She was telling someone, she didn't know who, that this was her fourth pregnancy and that she had lost the other three. The message reverberated in her head. *She had lost her other three children. Gone from her, left on a streak of lightning, a moonbeam. Stolen from her in the dark when she was not watching, as all children are stolen away from the source.* Effie felt hot tears on her face. In her dream, dark red blood ran down between her legs and pooled on the stark white floor. And this mystic fourth child of hers who was slipping away before she had a chance to hold the tiny speck of protoplasm; what was that? *Effie knew.* She grasped not her flat abdomen in reassurance but her solar plexus and pushed hard. Holding tight. Refusing to part, to release into the void this unborn child of her creation.

ɛ♦ɛ♦ɛ♦

Are you beginning to question the reliability of the narrative voice? It's all illusion, you know. Capturing the elusive element of surprise is one of the small satisfactions left us. To provide surprise requires moving beyond what is imagined, which is what the writer strives for, what the lover strives for.

"Structurally," the well-dressed woman writer might say, "this stinks."

Chapter Three

Effie recognized that her circumstances were not unique. On campuses the world over bright-eyed, intelligent, sincere women, women of all conformations—though the middle-aged were mostly notably susceptible—listened in rapt attention as pompous male professors prattled on ad nauseam (if one were honest), shared with overeager students their ideas on art, on literature, on the state of the world. Out of need, out of an inexpressible longing for an ineffable commodity, females came in search. By the hordes they came. By the droves. And they found there, waiting gleefully, the mentors, the vainglorious, whose traps were hidden and well-baited.

And what was the lure, the attraction? Most certainly not sex, although the nature of the intercourse was all encompassing. Mentors and students made love after hours in humanities offices; they fornicated in parked cars, or in hotels, although this practice was generally reserved for out-of-town conventions as many academics were notoriously cheap and disliked paying for something they could get for free.

You saw them in cafeterias holding court, often as not entertaining more than one admiring, trembling female. You saw them in hallways, in classes after hours, in cozy intimate restaurants that served espresso and catered to the veneration of the master.

An educated passerby might smile knowingly and dismiss the phenomenon of younger woman, antiquated academic as Electra attraction, but that explanation was simplistic and one-dimensional. What then, if not sex, if not Daddy recaptured, was the lure? What drew them *en masse*? Beautiful words, to be sure. The symbolic concretization of ideas. "It would not be inappropriate for us to talk of love," Walter had said. And into that Effie had read a descent into the region of the unknown. "Music helps," he told her, and by that she assumed he meant the sound that awakens the will, but perhaps he only meant pleasant noise to fuck by. If art is an organization of rhythms, Effie sought in their relationship themes to express the vision, while he sought the meter, the cadence of his pulsating prick. Ah, the poetry.

As an instructor herself, Effie was interested to note that the phenomenon did not usually work in reverse. She had her share of admiring, adulating young males who frequented her office, who asked if they could escort her to her car after dark, one who even ventured a request that she accompany him to the movies. (She declined.) They were sweet. They were cute. But they did not interest her. What was the difference? For one, and primary for her, Effie would not take advantage of her position as Walter did, to engage in relationships with students. And besides, for those embarked on a quest, the first encounter was always with a protective figure, a guide who offered advice. Walter as Wizard in the fairy tale? Was that the academic's attraction? Walter held the promise of a magical union with the sublime. He symbolized a relationship with the creative process.

The college for which she worked, a religious institution in the San Fernando Valley, frowned on unions of any kind unless they were carried out under the sanctity of holy matrimony. The joke around campus, where many forms of social fraternization were strictly prohibited, was that sex would lead to dancing.

Effie was baffled continually by the barrage of notes and flyers she found in her mailbox at work. *Join us for a talk on the feminists' view of Jesus. Learn about liberation theology and Christian Marxism.* She had yet to attend one of these seminars.

Despite the fact that the majority of faculty looked like television preachers, complete with bouffant hair, Effie nonetheless found the school much to her liking. They left her alone. They never questioned her teaching methods or unconventional approaches. As long as her student evaluations came back positive, she was kept on the roster part-time. Full-time positions went to members of the church.

A memorable story—she heard this from another instructor at another institution, who knew the man in question—concerned a full-time faculty member, who was, number one, Jewish, and number two, gay. This illustrious professor, before he came out, had at one time been married to a member of the church. Under his television-preacher costume it was rumored he wore a Star of David. Every time Effie saw him in the halls she smiled broadly, notification they shared a grand secret, were putting one over on the powers that be. As Walter had put one over on her.

Seduction, she discovered much later, was the name of the game Walter had played. *To lead astray by persuasion or false promises.* Walter was looking for another place to live, he assured her. He just hadn't found it yet.

❦❦❦

You know that sounds bitchy, a trite hard. The problem is that there is no reliable tradition of female narrators in modern fiction, modern being the late 1980s where Effie found herself residing. Women narrators are generally branded neurotic or mad or worse. Ideally, the character should act as though she feels things less deeply than the reader, thereby enabling the intelligent consumer of fiction to form her own opinion. The fashion today is for specificity, and you, alas, lean more toward summarization. Staying within the truth of the feeling is tricky business. You know Walter Rabinowitz behaved poorly but the reader wants to see this for herself. You want the reader to trust you; you were *there*.

❦❦❦

She sat at the kitchen table in her trailer and looked out to sea. On a good day when the smog was negligible she could see Catalina and Anacapa. On a good day. Not today. The work before her was responsible, in large part, for the frustration she felt. When her agent had called with an offer of a four-thousand-dollar contract for a one-hundred-and-sixty-page teenage detective novel, Effie said yes because she needed the money; it was that simple.

The book was not simple; the editors followed a format, a strict *bible* that drove Effie nuts. Initially she had decided if she were to partake in this writing-by-numbers that she would at least address an issue that interested her.

She developed an outline. She sent it off, and cringed when the editor called back to say, "Our teenage detective does not go after toxic-waste polluters. Write about something kids can relate to—bank robbers or smugglers. The big-wigs don't know from toxic waste. They go from Manhattan to the Hamptons."

"Tell them to swim in the Hudson! Tell them to fall in the East River!" She felt like shouting. (And kids relate to bank robbers? News to her.)

Later, Ramona was quick to point out that the publishing house in question was owned by a large oil conglomerate. So much for pollution as subject matter.

On her second go-round, Effie placed her young female sleuth in an old-age home, attempting to ascertain for the inhabitants who was absconding with their jewels. "Our detective cannot hang out with old people," the editor informed her. "Try again."

Her frustration mounted. Walter, a writer himself, found the entire situation amusing. "I'm sure you'll use this material somehow," he told her. "Perhaps in another novel. It all means something." For Effie, what it meant was a lousy way to earn four grand.

6♦6♦6♦

"He left the toilet seat up." Effie looked around Ramona's living room, studying the faces of the members of the writing group.

Ramona shook her head. Her long, graying curls caught the sunlight through the window. "A bad sign."

"It is?" Lucy clearly did not understand. "My husband always leaves the toilet seat up."

"Lucy, the second wave of the feminist movement was in large part about men leaving the toilet seat up. Where were you during the sixties?" Blythe asked.

Lucy looked hurt.

"She's too young to remember or to understand the significance of such a symbolic act," Effie said.

"Symbolic, my foot," Blythe added. "He just forgot."

"Forget is the wrong word for a Freudian subconscious act." Lucy looked at Ramona in complete bewilderment. "Oh, Lucy," Ramona said, "you're so young. In the sixties men who left the toilet seat up were typecast, branded if you will, declared by feminists in their attendant publications as acting out aggressive tendencies. In this symbolic gesture women read: one, a lack of concern for members of the female species who generally, though not always, possess a smaller derriere and therefore are much more likely to fall through to water's edge. It's passive-aggressive."

"At any rate," Effie added, "we sit down more."

"Secondly, in this subconscious Freudian act feminists read a territorial imperative not unlike the gesture that causes male dogs to christen every tree, thus making their boundaries known. "Look here, fellas," the canine says, "I was here first.""

"Isn't that stretching things a bit?" Lucy asked.

"Not if you've ever found yourself floating fanny first in Tidy Bowl." Ramona cocked one eyebrow.

"You could, of course, make a significant argument against the advisability of peeing in the dark, similar to spitting into the wind, which would be well taken, but which skirts the issue." Effie looked knowingly at Lucy.

"Magazines really spent time on this subject?" Lucy's eyes widened.

Ramona continued. "At the time, certain magazines were rife with questionnaires which were supposed to enable a women to *read* her lover. Question number one: *Does he leave the toilet seat up?* Question number two: *Who sleeps in the wet spot?*

"You're kidding! This was journalism?" Lucy looked at the other three. "And anyway, I'm always the one to get a towel. After sex, Barry doesn't move."

Ramona and Blythe and Effie exchanged a knowing glance."Rolls over and falls asleep, does he?" Blythe asked.

"Hmmn. Unless he's hungry."

"Gawd! Is this progress?" Ramona, who was a good twenty years older than Lucy, was not impressed. "The question for Effie, though, is what did you do about it?"

Effie answered. "I fell in."

"After that?"

"I reminded myself that water is a symbol of purification. What was I supposed to do?"

"Tell him."

"Tell the man who writes to me—*you, who give so very much, sustain things by what you say and what you write and what you feel, and it is enormously vital and wondrous to me that you exist*—tell that person he left the toilet seat up?"

"Oh, my goodness!" Lucy said. "He wrote that? That's so beautiful!"

Effie, smug, answered. "I know."

Ramona's face registered concern. "Tell him, Effie," she commanded.

"Tell him gently," offered Lucy.

That others may misunderstand highlights the fact that to the writer, words mean one thing; to the reader, they may mean something else entirely. The only way the writer creates is to pour his or her personal power into the creation: art as extension of the self. Seeing the final version as separate and apart from oneself is the ultimate step. But it's damn hard getting there, especially when the obstacles to love and creativity are often strategically placed by others.

Chapter Four

"I have quite a large bill here for dental work. Did you have some work done?" James rattled papers on the other end of the line. She imagined him as she had seen him for years, sitting at his desk surrounded by mounds of disorganization.

"I had to have a root canal," she said. "And a crown."

"Why didn't you tell me?"

"Why didn't I tell you? I'm supposed to call you up and say, 'Today I had a root canal?' I thought the insurance covered most of it. Send me whatever the balance is and I'll pay it. I never thought to change the address, okay?"

"I just would have like to have known about it, Effie. That's all." He sounded wounded. James' habit of always wanting to *talk about things* was one of the issues that annoyed her the most. What he meant by that was that *he* wanted to talk and she was supposed to listen. Sometimes he went on for forty-five minutes without a break. If she tried to interject, he brought the conversation right back to himself. On top of that, he demanded the most excruciating, gruesome details about her private life. When she had a bladder infection and told him the medicine she was taking made her pee orange, he had to look. When she got new contact lenses, he had to watch her put them in. He wanted to know about the process in exacting detail. James would have liked to have had another child now that father participation in the birth process was a big thing. Effie informed him that she had no intention of reproducing solely for his experience of *being there.* She had been there three times; mostly it just hurt a lot. It gave her a creepy feeling; James was always looking over her shoulder, displaying too much interest in her bodily functions. What the hell was that about?

She assumed it was his mother, who, out of some queasiness, some unassailable inhibitions sexual or otherwise, had never assuaged her son's natural curiosity. So now Effie had to deal with it. "I filled out the insurance forms," she told him. "I guess it didn't cover everything."

"You know how much a porcelain crown costs, Effie?"

"You want me to give it back, is that it? You think I can get a refund?"

"All I'm asking is that you keep me apprised of things, that's all."

"I certainly will. The dentist says my mouth is in fine shape. I'm still menstruating regularly. I take my vitamins. The dog does not have worms. My Creeping Charlie is blooming."

James sighed. "I'm interested because I care, Effie." For once she kept her mouth shut and did not respond with a remark about how much he must have been caring when he went to Mexico with another woman.

"Send me the bill, James. I don't expect you to pay for my root canal."

How she would pay was the question she asked herself after he hung up the phone. The snail-farm business a friend had suggested turned into a fiasco. She had spent thirty-five dollars for the initial order of snails, then eight more dollars for the cornmeal to cleanse their systems. The company was now requesting a huge shipping-and-handling fee to package the little critters and send them happily on their way to France where hungry people would chomp away on the snails raised by Effie. But before she could send off her shipping fees, one night the dog knocked the carton of snails off the counter and they escaped and ate most of her houseplants. So much for get-rich schemes. Ramona's "I told you so" rang in her ears.

She supposed she could write about it, turn the situation into a short story, or at very least, an article for a self-sufficiency magazine. Sometimes she felt like such a leech, sucking the blood out of experience, knowing that no matter what awful event happened to her, she would use it somehow. Friends said funny or sad or sensitive things to her and aside from her immediate genuine response, there lurked in the background another Effie already devising a plan whereby meaningful moments could be worked into stories that would sell. Exploitative, that's what she was. On the other hand, she sometimes suspected that her friends purposefully told her amusing incidents in the hope of eventually ending up in print. No one was genuine, without guile.

James was out of town for market week so Effie trotted back to the house to spend some time with the girls, even though the two were perfectly fine by themselves. She suspected they even enjoyed being on their own. She certainly could relate to that. Effie's son, Tim, had recently married and lived out of state. Megan, in her third year at state college, was busy with boys, classes, sorority sisters. Mandy had begun her first semester at a local junior college.

The yard was a mess. Weeds grew between her flowers in the rock garden. Effie would never have allowed such a state of affairs. Her flowers were her sustenance. She blamed James, not rationally, of course; she knew he didn't have time for frivolities such as flowers, yet on some subterranean level she knew he was letting the garden go on purpose. Passive-aggressive? Or to lure her back? She grabbed a weed and yanked. The damn thing broke in half, refused to relinquish its tentative hold on the earth. It's all so tentative, Effie thought. She gave up and went inside.

It made her feel sick to come back to the house. James had no sense of detail, of composition. She'd known that for years, of course, but with her around to act as buffer, it wasn't as noticeable. But now...things fell apart so easily.

She removed the green towels from the blue bathroom and hung them where they belonged, in the bathroom painted sea foam. But first she had to take the blue towels down. It hurt her to see everything in such a state of disrepair. James, too, was in such a state. It showed in his eyes. The man mooned around with a hound-dog look on his face that made her feel most uncomfortable. On the other hand, under the circumstances, she couldn't exactly expect him to be cheery.

Oh, it was all so absurd, so silly even. She wished she could get angry, but the feeling just would not materialize.

How could she justify anger over what was basically a different way of doing things? If only he didn't persist in storing the booze with the Mylanta.

Effie studied the cupboard hoping to find within its recesses some answer, but the dark interior revealed nothing. She could rearrange things. She definitely had the urge to reconstruct order out of the chaos James had made of the house in just a few short months.

She sighed and shut the pantry door. He might become angry once he noticed her hand in things. She had to acknowledge that in this house, at least, she no longer had a hand in things.

Effie proposed a light dinner for the girls, losing herself in the comfort of the kitchen. "Why is the vinegar in the refrigerator?" she asked Mandy, who sat at the table doing homework.

"I dunno. That's where Dad keeps it." Mandy looked up from her calculus book. Effie stared at the bottle. Perhaps the secret to the inner workings of her husband's mind were contained therein.

Effie imagined James reading some article on how the shelf life of vinegar was prolonged if stored in a cool place. She knew of no such study, but James was always pointing out things like that to her. Tidbits, he called them. "Did you know?" he'd begin, looking up from a magazine, proclaiming some nugget of information Effie had assimilated months, if not years, before.

"Is that so?" she learned to say, which struck her as less emasculating than "I already knew that." Was she missing his tidbits? She couldn't decide.

"Mom, you're wasting energy." Megan eyed the open refrigerator.

Mandy asked her sister to hand her an apple. Megan reached into the fruit bowl, grabbed an apple and tossed it to Mandy.

Effie looked up. "Good catch!" She shut the refrigerator door. "How about a quiche for dinner, and a salad, girls? Seems to be fixings enough for that."

Mandy shrugged. "Whatever."

For hours the image of the vinegar in the refrigerator stayed with Effie. She found this separation business fascinating; she was learning more about James away from him than she had in his company. After twenty-six years of marriage, did people have to live apart in order to become whole once more?

Chapter Five

You keep thinking about what the well-dressed woman writer said about Effie being a hateful bitch. It takes courage to be a writer, to be an artist of any sort. Oftentimes you miss the mark; in fact, you may never get it right, although you strive to come close, to understand. If there is not room to honor the writer's intention, then what is the point?

For years Effie had found solace in the hills, took refuge in solitary glades away from the noise and bustle of family life. Now that she lived alone, away from both the joys as well as the confinements of motherhood, she increased her daily walks, sought the inner peace that her private haunts afforded. It was not unusual for her to spend two or three hours hiking, or for her to lose all sense of time watching the red-tailed hawks, or the coyotes. She knew the location of a fox den, as did the dog. She could identify a weasel's home. She surprised owls in the morning hours, woke them, sent them complaining on untimely flight. She could flush out deer, a skill of dubious value unless one felt, as she did, that the splendid sight of a doe was reward enough.

Her walks were her meditation. She had tried other methods, had sought to still her mind through concentration, through rapt attention to her own inner music. But the moments she achieved the *oversoul* always took place outdoors, were always in harmony with the earth. She desired not to live *on* the land, but rather live in conjunction with the source that sustained and nourished her.

She had hoped to share this love with her children. Carefully, she taught them the names of the native wildflowers and the trees. She made up games, challenged them to look closely at the world, to see what others missed. And yet it had been Effie and not her children who spent enraptured moments studying the pollywogs they kept in an aquarium on the kitchen counter. She was the one who had stood by transfixed, watching.

She became acquainted with the toads in her garden, recognized them as individuals: the fat one, the shy one, the talker. Toads, she was pleased to note, made friendly beeping noises when she ran water down the gopher holes they sometimes called home.

Even the ground squirrels, which were the bane of serious gardeners, provided entertainment. Even though they ate her vegetables, she still found them enchanting. "Think of them as rats with furry tails," a neighbor told her, and proceeded to bait traps in her own yard, a process that made Effie flinch with outrage. When Effie's dog killed a nursing female, and the babies crawled out of their den in desperation, Effie was right there feeding them, letting them crawl all over her. She spent hours on her belly in the dust mothering rodents, animals that would subsequently destroy her garden.

Her children were suspicious of these activities. James, too, had shaken his head, although he emerged a few moments later with a camera in hand to record the photos of their newfound family.

She had sought to give but one thing to her offspring: a childhood to remember. The experience was not without effort. They had planted a huge garden, which Effie recognized much later was her attempt to recapture her own childhood, those wondrous times in her grandmother's backyard picking tomatoes and raspberries. While she had been enamored of the garden, her children balked and protested. "Do we have to plant more beans? I hate beans. The mosquitoes are biting me. Can I go in now?" What for Effie had been a heaven, was for her brood, a hell, one manufactured by their mother. What had gone wrong? In attempting to bring the past to the present what do we lose along the way? Effie didn't recall mosquitoes in her grandmother's garden, though most certainly there must have been. She didn't recall perspiring or moaning or the backbreaking toil of hoeing weeds. Memory is selective.

The goats they raised had been Effie's love. Initially the girls had found them cute; her son had found them mildly entertaining, and James found them a responsibility that tied the family to the property. Twice a day Effie had milked the does, made cheese and yogurt, and fought with her children to drink the milk. Being an earth mother was a full-time occupation, one for which her enthusiasm was not shared. Perhaps what she sought to create was not so much a perfect childhood for her kids, but rather a recreated childhood for herself.

They had fresh eggs from their chickens, and while the store-bought variety could not compare with the delightful brown orbs laid by her Rhode Island Reds, still no one had warned her about the attendant flies or the fact that establishing a pecking order was more than a cliché.

The ponies the children rode and curried and loved had also been missing from Effie's girlhood, though she recalled ever so distinctly having been desirous of one. She was charmed by their equine antics and their warm presence, perhaps even more than the girls.

James sighed a great deal and shook his head as each arrival vied for position in the barnyard. He delighted in sharing with the business community amusing tales from the home front: how a goat had learned to butt open the sliding-glass door with its horns and how it sneaked into the house for bananas off the kitchen table; how, before the completion of the chicken coop, twenty baby chicks lived in the bathtub; how a mouse set up housekeeping under the hood of his car. He liked having Effie at home doing what good earth mothers do. And more. And for years, the demands of young children and extended home kept her busy and content.

Yet one can talk to goats for only so long, especially if the earlier call of literature goes unheeded. Which was when Effie returned to school for another master's degree. Which was when she decided to concentrate on her writing. Then, having established some success for herself, she decided to join yet a larger group of similarly like-minded writers and so returned for more post-grad work. Which was how she met Walter.

You find writing immensely comforting because it is the one place where things are focused. The knowledge that you are responsible for beginnings as well as for endings brings satisfaction because in life, as opposed to art, there is no way to determine if one is headed toward a climactic moment or whether in fact, one has just experienced the denouement. It is always in retrospect that matters achieve clarity. In fiction, things have shape. In art, emotions coincide with the event. In life, circumstance and feeling do not always correspond.

You were going to write about the romantic myth that leaves women believing if they find their dream man, their soul mate, that they will never feel separate again. You were going to write that the myth is a lie. Only, so what? One can do nothing about what exists in the realm of myth except perhaps expose the truth, and that so few women want to believe the truth leaves you—or Effie—creating stories for a very limited audience..

Naturally Effie has to sigh a great deal and in despair put away her paper and pen. Some days you wonder why you bother.

The interior of Ramona's house reminded Effie of a fern grotto she had once seen in Hawaii. Wide-leafed plants inhabited every corner; greenery hung from the ceiling. On the tabletops African violets blossomed in profusion. Coleus, radiating health, brightened windowsills. Effie loved plants as well, but Ramona's overactive green thumb made her a bit nervous; wasn't there only so much oxygen per cubic foot? She knew plants gave off good stuff, but in the process was it possible they were using up her share of some vital substance? It was only after knowing Ramona for some time that she was able to relax amongst the forest: Ramona appeared to bear no ill effects from her continuous relationship with the ferny things, so Effie had to assume all was well.

"Some herb tea?" Ramona moved with a certain natural style that Effie admired.

"Yes, that would be nice. Thank you."

"How are things on the mountain?"

"Things are fine. The girls spent the night. We went for a long hike, then baked cookies afterward. It felt like old times. Yes, everything's fine, except..." Effie drank her tea and shared with her friend her tale of woe, watching as Ramona's eyes widened.

"Let me get this straight." Ramona stared at her in disbelief. "You left behind your husband of over twenty-five years, a man who adores you beyond reason, a man who would do anything for you, for some schmuck who can't get it up?"

Effie winced. "Technically, that's not correct, on both counts. James doesn't just adore me, he smothers me. 'I don't want to destroy your spirit,' he said. On some level I think that's exactly what he wants. No, the other one. How can I put this nicely, without offending sensibilities?"

"Whose sensibilities?" Ramona asked. "The dog's?"

"All right. It's just that by the time I'm getting started, he's finished. As in final."

"Good God, Effie. There are other ways."

"You know that. I know that. James knows that. Walter appears not to. Or doesn't care. This is not something I've had a great deal of experience with. So, the question is, what do I do about it?"

"Have you tried a few...ah...persuasive techniques?"

"I've tried standing on my head, tap dancing, singing 'Ode to Joy.' There is no raising Lazarus from the dead. Finished is finished."

Ramona laughed.

"Excuse me, friend, but I don't happen to find this all so amusing." Effie glared at Ramona.

"Did you really expect to find yourself an aging sex maniac?"

"I don't know what I expected. Closeness. Tenderness. Waking up next to him. Rolling over to find him there. But he won't spend the night. If he spent the night we could try again in the morning." Effie looked as though she might cry. "Do you suppose he takes his teeth out or something? Maybe he gives himself nightly enemas?"

"Effie, bail out of this."

"But I love him!" She wailed.

"Do you have any idea how masochistic that sounds?"

"Damn it, I am not masochistic! Is it masochistic to care for someone? Women learn to put other people's needs before their own and the thanks we get, even from other women, is that we are called masochists." Effie crossed her arms over her chest.

"Ramona thought about this. "You're right. I apologize."

Effie continued. "Try thinking of yourself first and then what happens? Guilt, with a capital G. It's a no-win, Ramona. I think his problem has to do with all the other obligations he brings to bed with him."

"Or the other women. I've known the type, Effie. Pretty soon it gets really crowded between the sheets. But, dear heart, it's just as easy to love one that works the way you want it to."

"Oh, you're so cold, Ramona! And anyway, it wasn't sex that pulled me to him."

"Listen, gal," Ramona said. I didn't spend five years in therapy, two more in group, and all of the seventies in the women's movement for nothing. What all this boils down to is taking care of yourself, survival instinct if you will, and right now I don't see you taking very good care of yourself. So tell me, if it wasn't sex, what was it?"

"It was, it was...." Effie thought a moment. "It was pretty words. I fell in love with pretty words."

"Oh, for gawd's sake!"

"But it's true. He was someone who understood words. And through that I found a connection." Effie paused. "Or thought I did. And how well are you surviving, Ramona?"

Ramona shrugged. Ramona's husband, an arrogant artist Effie found difficult to like or even admire, had six years ago run away with a doe-eyed Polynesian girl who was twenty-five years his junior. Ramona still clung to the romantic notion of his imminent return, although for the life of her, Effie could not figure out why. Most certainly Ramona was better off without him. Most certainly Ramona had blossomed artistically as well as personally since his departure.

Effie played with her teacup. "I read the other day that in order to achieve Nirvana one has to give up three things: desire, delusion, and hostility."

"I could give up desire," Ramona said. "Never delusion. Hostility would be difficult as well." After all these years Ramona was still able to work up considerable anger toward her ex-husband.

"I could give up hostility before desire. Maybe it's not desire so much as passion—passion for life, the intensity of the moment. Delusion, now that strikes me as next to impossible."

"I guess neither one of us gets to Nirvana, at least this time round."

"If I could give up desire," Effie mused, "it wouldn't make much difference about Walter's notional...equipment."

Ramona pulled a brown leaf off a fern. "Maybe that's not desire. Maybe that's just sex. Effie, you need to broaden your horizons."

"Broaden my horizons, as in men? And where are these guys supposed to come from? Number one, it's not that easy. Number two, I'm not sure I'm ready. I may never be ready."

"What about your writing class? Aren't there a few possibilities there?"

"In my class," Effie told her, "there are three men. One is a twenty-nine-year-old drug addict. One is a nice-looking fellow who chose the seminar as an opportunity to come out of the closet, to explore his true nature with words. Number three is an older gentlemen I might have found interesting, only he has the hots for another member of the class, who I think might be all of twelve."

"I hear you."

"It's all so depressing. I've decided I don't need a man. I need help coping. You're right about that."

"Does the writing help?"

"Sure it helps. It saved my life. Now I need to figure out what to do with the rest of it."

"Perhaps you should see someone."

"Perhaps I should."

The someone Effie chose to see was Julie. Effie had taken the therapist's name from a list given to her by the counseling office at the college where she was employed. During their initial phone conversation Effie discovered several connections. Julie was also a writer, having published a book on codependency. Julie also had an intuitive understanding of the creative process, of what it meant to be a woman artist. Many of her clients came to her, seeking a cure for writer's block.

Mostly what Effie responded to was Julie's warmth and genuine good humor. It seemed to Effie that Julie hid little in terms of what she was thinking, perhaps not a positive trait in a therapist, but one which Effie admired because she thought it reflected Julie's honest approach to life and her willingness to confront issues head-on. Of course it was always easier to confront someone else's issues head-on, but even here, Julie shared a bit of her own trials.

Effie appreciated that Julie was willing to share a lot of things, mostly Effie's pain and confusion. Together they searched for answers not readily available. Together they searched for ways to uncover the inner obstacles to creativity, to love.

Chapter Six

You believe that passionate love is a way to the divine. You continually seek a way to your own transformation. The commitment to make an inward journey, to face the death of the old self in order to encounter a new feminine spirit is your heroic quest. You are challenged to unlock the doors of your inner self. You know that possessiveness, expectations, are major obstacles to love. "Give up your expectations and you have all things," said the Buddha. (Effie notes that the Buddha was not married.)

The difficulty, you've discovered, is that it is damn hard to live all the time on the spiritual plane. One has to eat. One has to work.

Walter had once asked Effie if she were anorexic. The answer was no; she loved to eat. She was naturally thin because of metabolic rate and because of an active physical schedule. Nonetheless, his question prompted her to think that it would be very nice if humans could live on nothing but air, devour knowledge instead of french fries. If one could fill up on the smell of grass and wild roses and earth after a rain, perhaps it would be possible to live eternally in the spiritual realm. Once, years before, in the sixties, she and James had picked up a hitchhiker on the way to San Francisco. After several hours of driving, they stopped at a coffee shop. James offered to buy the young man something to eat. "I don't eat," the stranger replied, "I live on air."

Effie had been glad to see him go; he had been an odd one and he smelled awful. But the thought remained, intrigued her so that sometimes she contemplated a world where everyone lived on air.

She had originally seen Walter as part of the process of achieving inner harmony and balance. What she was to discover was that only she could give that to herself. Still, she felt with him a magical communion, an ability to talk without speaking, an ability to see beyond the mysterious recesses of herself. She thought of him as her guide leading her toward creativity. But one night she realized that this ghostly lover of hers was indeed, an unobtainable love.

"What happened to the other student?" she asked him. She took his glasses off to kiss his face.

"I guess she got tired of waiting around for me to leave Ruth."

"She waited three and a half years, Walter. That's a long wait."

He became defensive. "I can't leave the woman who has spent thirty years of her life with me with nothing."

Effie spoke gently. "You talk of financial burdens, yet it seems to me you are tied to debts of another sort." Sadness overwhelmed her as did the recognition that a daily relationship with this man was impossible. How had she succumbed? She had believed him. "All I ask of you," she had said at the onset, "is that you be honest with me."

"The question," he replied, "is whether I am honest with myself."

If Walter had been for her an ideal, one who promised the experience of the divine, maybe she too had fulfilled a similar function in his life. He dwelled in a fantasy world and perhaps also sought a romanticized love, which was possible only in another realm. She recognized if she were to escape the pull of the phantom lover, she had to quit projecting her own creativity onto him. She had to quit longing for the extraordinary and endowing Walter with the power to lead her where she had to lead herself.

So now what? At least it hadn't taken her three and a half years to figure out. But it didn't hurt less. Love knows no time frame.

And demands no return.

෬ ෬ ෬

"You, my friend, are joining me for an evening of intellectual stimulation. Plus, perhaps we'll meet some new people."

"I'm game. Where are we going?"

"To a seminar on eco-feminism," Ramona replied.

"Eco-feminism. Women who sit around discussing temperature-controlled compost?"

"No, silly. Women who discuss how the patriarchal society has forgotten its biological connection with nature, with women, and with other people. We'll be exploring ways to dismantle the process of domination."

"Lots of luck with that!"

Ramona said, "It's a nonviolent process, using ritual, politics, etc., as tools to effect change."

"The last time I looked, the political arena was not exactly nonviolent."

"Do you want to come or not?"

"All right, I'll tag along. But promise me, if it turns out to be nothing but a bunch of women fertilizing the lawn with menstrual blood, we're leaving."

ᏕᎯᏕᎯᏕᎯ

Ramona and Effie tromped off to the lecture to learn about how the estrangement from nature began with the removal of the goddess. Effie listened as bright, articulate people discussed what she believed all along—that chance encounters were not chance but rather bridges to the miraculous, a way to move closer to unseen forces.

She looked around at the gathered crowd, which for her was a delightful time trip back to the sixties. Long-haired men and barefoot, braless women joined ranks with the well-dressed and with the politically astute. "I would have worn my Birkenstocks," she told Ramona, "only the dog ate them. Which is what happens to aging hippies. Now that we can afford to buy ninety-dollar sandals, the dog eats them."

"The fragmentary worldview, the separation between the natural world and the spiritual world, is in great part responsible for the cosmic mess we find ourselves experiencing today. The patriarchal system seeks not to live within the universe, but to run and to control it."

"This speaker is on to something," Effie whispered. She listened, fascinated, as the lecturer continued to elaborate on the feminine viewpoint, one in which the center of the universe was relationship-oriented: relationship with other people, relationship with the self, relationship with the earth mother.

The lecturer spoke of power as if she were speaking of love—a commodity that was limitless because when it was shared, it expanded. Shared power increased power. Power had nothing to do with control. Effie thought of Walter, of James. Though she was capable of understanding what the speaker was saying, she wondered how they would have responded. The world as we know it, she thought, is composed of those who speak two different languages: male and female. So who was supposed to translate? No wonder relationships were so complex.

The final speaker was a Peruvian woman who shared indigenous views of the universe, which were compatible with the eco-feminist position. But when the woman suggested the audience get in touch with themselves, Effie balked. "Say hello to your bodies," the woman intoned. "Introduce yourself to your toes. Say hello to your ankles."

Effie felt very silly greeting her toes. Plus, she found the process exacting and time consuming.

"Enter through your rectum and greet your internal organs."

"Hey," Effie nudged Ramona, "isn't she getting just a little bit personal?" Ramona giggled and gestured for Effie to be quiet.

"Say hello to your intestine."

"Ramona," Effie whispered, "this could take all night. We have twenty-seven feet of intestine!"

The two women exited the auditorium while the speaker in her melodious voice, directed the audience to "say hi to your heart. Embrace your bosom."

Effie and Ramona walked out into the cool night air. "If I could get to the point where embracing my own bosom was sustaining, I'd feel I had arrived." Effie squeezed her arms over her chest. "Nope, it just doesn't do it. For some reason, it feels better when a man does the embracing. Does that mean there's something wrong with me? Damn it all to hell."

Ramona attempted the same experiment. Effie watched as her friend hugged herself, then sighed, "I know just what you mean. Damn it all to hell."

᪥᪥᪥

The next day, in an effort to get out of her own skin and to do something productive, Effie called her daughters and together they went to the animal shelter where they volunteered and walked the homeless dogs. She wished she could bring all of the canines home; their companionship, however brief, sheltered her.

Chapter Seven

After Walter's acknowledgment that he had no intention of
leaving the home front, Effie deliberated. If she stayed in the
relationship, she was a fool, a woman who was not taking care
of herself. There was bound to be distortion: Love had already
changed to disillusionment, ecstasy to nightmare. She didn't
want things out of balance, and she had seen, too often,
relationships that began with an intense attraction turn into a
battlefield where the couple ended up devouring each other.

That her feelings were not primarily sexual was a
realization on her part. The connection, for Effie at least, went
beyond the spoken or written word. (Or did it? What was it
she had projected onto this man?) The connection was
something she *felt*, a connection that could not be investigated
on any rational level: It just *was* and she felt it had to be
considered. She suspected Walter felt it as well, or here again,
was she merely fooling herself? If she, as a writer, could
master this confusion, she felt she would gain new ground.
Three steps forward and two steps back.

Walter suggested they might have known each other in
past lives; his spiritual quest led him in directions she did not
quite understand, but who was she to judge? Effie tried to
write about how she felt, about her communion with her
ghostly lover, but the words betrayed her. It was a sense of
fusion, of union from the inner core outward, a beginning
within that permeated and charged the entire atmosphere
surrounding them. It was a desire to crawl inside his head; it
was not being able to get close enough.

And no wonder! How does one become close with
someone who is rarely around? She stared at her words,
symbols of her longing to unite. Love had never been like this
before; she felt a presentiment of sorts. Of course she
recognized that sounded quite ridiculous and premeditated and
that no one would believe such a thing. It was not a conscious
recognition so much as an affirmation of something
simmering beneath the surface waiting to bubble, waiting to

be. If Walter had recognized it as well, he had called it other, more recognizable names.

In the beginning she had written to him that he was a rare find, like the perfect skipper she had searched for for hours on the pebbly shore of the Ottawa River. It was the weight and shape and feel of the stone that suggested possibility. And when she picked up such a stone, she knew; even at ten- years- old, she knew.

And once she found her stone, she didn't want to let it go. It was enough to hold it, to admire it, knowing that her discovery could outdo the rest. The other kids, motivated by instinct, perhaps envy, knew too. They prodded her to throw her skipper, toss her prize. She bore their taunts and dares, knowing she did not have to prove anything. Instead, she slipped her treasure into her river-stained-shorts' pocket, and the weight of her discovery so close to her skin, brought untold happiness. She trotted off to her grandmother's cottage and smiled with joy when the old woman studied her find, then proclaimed solemnly, "Looks like a good one."

She missed her pebble-skipping grandmother, who gave her summers to remember. Could it be that Effie, greedy, had just taken them—caught fish and dove off logs on their way to the sawmill—rowed unattended too near the rapids; spied, warm summer evenings, on teenage neckers parked on the shore and wondered what that was all about. She hooked arms with the girl next door and plodded down the river path singing, "I Am the Happy Wanderer." The neighbor girl had been a far better singer, but Effie was louder.

She longed to return to that shore. Instead, she sat at pond's edge—a magical place in the mountains—amongst the cattails and watched the coots follow each other over the water, listened to them make reassuring duck noises. And she felt the poke and prod of the reeds as she leaned against them. The dragonflies played there, danced there. She watched as they drew flame. Red ones. Orange ones. Iridescent blue ones. Effie thought she might die from the sight of it. Sometimes a great blue heron stopped by for a frog or an unknown fishy dinner and that, too, pleasured her.

As Walter had pleasured her. Because he understood about dragonflies. Because he was moonstruck and notional and because he flew kites and dreamed in Technicolor.

Effie's ability to ferret out what was operational in certain scenes, or settings, was the result of functioning by intuition—a scary business. She discovered in her relationship with Walter that intensity of feeling could mask the essential truth of things. Finally, however, a light bulb had gone on and clarity shined on muddied waters, waters muddied by her as she rushed forward, not giving things time to settle. She couldn't help rushing headlong, comet-like, at him, at life. And while she recognized that haste and impatience were destructive, still her enthusiasm always resulted in the big shove.

As a child on the river she learned that patience was the virtue that was rewarded by delicious fish nibbles on her toes. Go slowly; wait until the sun glitters through the shallows, and the minnows return. Eventually the fish adjust to your shadow.

Somewhere along the way she had discarded that lesson of her girlhood. The desire to reach out, to discover, to *feel* superseded and soon she was running again, losing too much along the way. Her sadness was wanting to experience so much with Walter and seeing it was not to be.

Effie was trying to be alone. She was trying to let go of situations that were not good for her, that brought not satisfaction, but sadness. She considered long and hard whether the experience of Walter, not any expectation of him as emotional support, but simply the experience of him, was worth the confusion. The answer was clouded because he was not an ordinary man.

Her inner core of security was tested by the new situation in which she found herself circling. Sometimes it was hard. And frightening. The trick was balancing selfhood with the very real desire to share the miraculous. She had discovered she did not require someone by her side in order to feel joyous and whole. But it certainly was sweeter that way. It made sense that way, as much sense as anything made.

Effie wrote him a letter. And as she wrote, she raged. Hot tears spilled onto the page, smearing her efforts, blurring edges. In her relationship with him, the edges had always been blurred.

She is trying so hard, Walter, so damn hard. She wants him to succeed, wants him to find the joy and peace he is seeking. She would have liked to have enhanced those possibilities. She wants to give the best of herself, but those needs are too often thwarted.

She has immense capacity for understanding, but she also has needs and wants that are not met in this relationship. She is no longer willing to relinquish all rights to what she wants. She has to love herself first and she is tired of feeling frustrated and disappointed. She is not willing to sacrifice the now for a future that never comes. She is not willing to sacrifice part of herself, the part that has more to give than he allows.

She has been thinking a lot about point of view. Everyone is right and everyone acts correctly according to his or her point of view. Maybe we got stuck in limited omniscient. It's her fault, too; she never learned to be properly casual. She wishes she were different, but she's not. She can't subtract but she knows the score. The score is more heartache than happiness. She knows too that he is a gift and that as a result, she is better than before: richer.

It wasn't the bafflement, Walter. It was the connection, the point of intersection, even if it was only in her head. It was the intuitive understanding without words—the secret smile between two ravaged hearts.

He did lead her to places never before visited...

There are a lot of things she can't do right now: blow bubbles, watch kites soar, walk in Sycamore Park. She can't look at barrel cactus. She no longer asks the dog to heel. And she doesn't listen to Mozart or classical guitar or the Eagles, because she's been to the limit...

She hopes he finds the "it" he's searching for. She hopes the mother of the universe watches over him. She hopes he knows how grateful she is that for her, he did indeed, make a difference.

❧ ❧ ❧

For two days Effie sat with the letter, wondering why she had written it in third person. She toyed with the idea of tearing it up. On the third day, exhausted, despairing, she mailed the missive. Then she came home and wrote a poem about how unavailable men were attractive because they *were* unavailable. Like Daddy, who never meant to be.

Chapter Eight

Her father had been a yarn spinner—a teller of tales—a brilliant man, a lover of illusion. And she had believed his fantasies—all of them—bought into his realm of the imagination, as later she bought into the magic of Walter's words because she needed to believe. It wasn't until her father's death that she came to know the truth, an awakening that brought with it the realization that for all her life she had lived a fantasy, had lived in a world of her father's creation. Perhaps if she had had a mother to protect her from the ravages of the fairy tale, her life might have been different. But her mother left on the wing, departed when Effie was five and was not seen again.

Effie, as a youngster, was seen by adults as a sylph; they often commented on her ethereal nature. And her favorite childhood stories, aside from her father's tales of adventure and high humor, were about elves, brownies, imps who visited in the night and went about their mischief, disappearing at dawn's first light. She loved diaphanous-winged fairies who lived under toadstools and who drank from dew-soaked flower petals.

Effie grew up in Southern California, though considered Canada her spiritual home. It was never explained fully how they landed in California; she thought it was her father's earliest attempts to please her mother, to give her jewelry and a car and a house in the suburbs. And then when her mother left, and the money did too, Effie and her father were the residual effects, the oily scum where the water recedes, two lost souls amongst the flotsam.

Until lately she had never thought about how it must have been for him, raising a child alone, a girl child, and doing the best he could, though sometimes getting it wrong. The greatest wrong—and she was not to learn of this until after his death—was keeping her mother from her. She would never know whether he was motivated by her best interest or by a desire to hurt the woman who left him and ran back to her first husband.

On her thirtieth birthday, she began a search for her mother; she searched in earnest for the woman who existed in memory, who had loved flowers and dogs. But Effie found her too late. Her mother lay dying in a hospital in Toronto, her liver rotted away from the effects of one too many attempts to ease the pain—the final pain being the loss of a second child, who after her mother's third divorce chose to live with her father. By the time Effie winged her way to Ontario, her mother was gone.

If she had difficulty accepting the passing of a woman she hardly knew, she had a harder time accepting that the all-powerful force in her life was not immortal. That year she refused to believe in death, refused to see the weakened laboring man as receding from her. By that time she had a husband and a baby—a few weeks old—to hold on to. And she had her father's stories. Until she learned the truth.

᠍᠍ᡀ᠍ᡀᡀ

She was surprised to see so many Chinese in attendance. When they passed by the mahogany casket holding her father's body, they bowed. It was this simple elegant gesture of final respect that drew reaction; if only she could have bowed simply and been absolved.

Effie did not notice that James was there beside her until he reached over and squeezed her hand. She returned the gesture, a kindness given for a kindness received, although she did not find his presence reassuring.

They were in the chapel and she was crying not so much for a father departed as for words left unspoken. They had separated the family from the rest of the mourners and except for James, Effie would have preferred to sit on the other side of the gauzy sheet, thin protection from what ailed her.

After the service the minister handed her the jade ring her father always wore, the ring her father bought in Hong Kong. She slipped it over her thumb. It was the only appendage that approximated a fit, but, of course here, too, the remembrance slipped and twisted. Her father's hands were large, giant warriors that had thrown her skyward while she shrieked with pretend terror. Only once did those giants flail out in anger. The bruise still sat on her soul.

In a grey limousine three of them rode to the gravesite. Effie looked out the tinted window. The spring flowers that lined the cemetery's narrow winding roadway were all a dingy yellow wash. The children frolicking beside the small lake, and the greedy ducks they fed, were a bilious hue. The color made her feel dizzy, as though the passing sights were part of some crazy dreamscape.

At the gravesite the chauffeur pulled in behind the hearse. He opened Effie's door. It was late May and a blast of unseasonable heat greeted them as they emerged from the car: first Effie, then James, then Effie's father's first wife. She was not her mother. She was not anything to her except the person who told her it would be all right to wear pink to the funeral. Effie was the only one so dressed and she was embarrassed, but more embarrassed by the thin warm milk that had begun to leak from her breasts. Her infant son had been left behind so that she might say a proper goodbye. Only Effie knew it was too late for proper goodbyes.

She concentrated on the hot tingling sensation inside her overburdened breasts. It seemed unduly appropriate that what nourishment she could offer was withheld on this day.

The attendants had set up seven chairs at the gravesite, but only the three of them sat down. The other family members stood, and the division this created was no worse than the gap that had existed between them for some while, now accommodated for all to see.

The sun was blinding and Effie was glad she had remembered to bring her sunglasses. She listened to more droning words. She twirled the ring on naked fingers, each one in turn. By the time the casket was lowered into its cement jacket, she had a piercing headache.

They escaped to the awaiting limousine, leaving other family members to accept the condolences of weeping friends. From the safety of the car, she watched her aunt assume the proper position, offering a dainty hand to an old acquaintance. The mourners did as expected and passed by her, the dutiful guests in a receiving line.

The chauffeur pulled the car away from the curb. Effie glanced down at the rolled sticky pamphlet she had been clinging to since the service. She tried smoothing the creased paper; though the wrinkles remained, she could still read the print. Reacting to what she read, she giggled. "Look," she told James. "He's resting in space C-1121. They've lined him up with all the rest."

His father's first wife spoke gently. "You must be tired."

Effie slumped back against the seat. "I was thinking of all the people we should have notified. The people of a lifetime."

James reached over and squeezed her hand. "The important ones know."

She longed for air. The cool substitute that flowed through the vents did little to sustain her. She shivered, though perspiration clung to the back of her dress. "Did he ever tell you about the lady in green?" She asked her father's first wife.

"What lady in green?"

"In Russia. She had green hair and green eyes and dressed only in green. Green everything." Effie closed her eyes, visualizing her father with this exotic creature.

There was a horrible pause. "Your father was never in Russia."

Effie looked directly at her. "Yes, he was. Before he married you. Way before. Before he in lived in Hong Kong."

The answer came slowly. "Your father never lived in Hong Kong."

Blood vessels in her head pounded. Black lights behind her eyes throbbed. *All those nights she sat on his knee, his good one, and listened enraptured as he described foreign people, events, places.*

"You mean *none* of it was true?"

The other woman nodded. Effie searched for her husband's hand and squeezed. "But why?"

"I asked your grandmother that years ago, when I first realized he was...fabricating."

"Lying, you mean."

"To him it wasn't lying. To him, it was real. All of it."

"Grandma knew as well?" She tried to recall her grandmother's placid face listening to her father's stories. "But *why*?"

"Your grandmother was responsible. At least she never stopped encouraging him. She felt sorry for him, I suppose, because of the polio."

When Effie was a little girl she used to walk in front of him, pretending she wasn't with him, pretending she didn't know the man with the awful limp.

"Your grandmother told me that as a child your father used to sit on the curb and watch all the other children playing. He couldn't join in, but he would sit there for hours, watching. Just watching. That's when he made up the stories, incredible tales, even then." She paused. "I guess after a while both of them stopped noticing the difference between fact and fiction."

"But everyone believed him. All his friends...family." Effie looked at her quickly. "My aunt, did she know?"

The first wife nodded.

"And my mother?"

"I suppose so."

"But they never said anything."

Her father's first wife thought about this. "Perhaps they needed to believe, too."

Effie was glad when the limousine pulled up in front of the house where she once lived, now temporarily occupied by a stranger who knew more of her father than she. They were invited in but declined, pleading a need to return to their son. The need was real enough.

The two drove in silence. When they were almost home, she dared to speak. "Did you believe him?"

"Always." James' handsome face was luminous in the half light of approaching dark.

"I wonder why she told me. She ruined him for me."

"Because she made him real?"

Effie started to cry. "It was a purposeful, hateful act."

"You needed to know."

"Did I?"

He looked at her so tenderly that she wanted to enfold herself within him, a bumblebee enclosed and protected by the fragile petals of a summer rose.

🐝🐝🐝

Her son nuzzled his downy head against her breast, rooting for the nourishment she so gladly gave. She marveled at his funny tufted hairdo and the perfect half-moon nail on each minuscule finger. Her husband watched the two of them, then joined them finally in their warm nest of covers. It was a long time before he spoke. "Can you forgive him?"

"That's not the problem."

"Forgiving yourself?"

The tears started slowly, spilled over one by one onto silken baby hair. She was crying for the man she never knew, for the family that protected him even from himself. She took the giant jade ring from her thumb and placed it on the scratched nightstand. Someone had suggested to her that it would make a wonderful brooch, but she knew it must always remain as it was: an absolute reminder of the gentle hands that bore her upward.

Somewhere between his wondrous toss and the little-girl knowledge that flight is but momentary, lay perfect possibility. He gave her that land of illusion where happiness exploded in a mist of pure white light.

She got up, placing her sleeping son in his bassinet. He snorted and snuffled with infant satisfaction. Perhaps in baby dreams he too had found it—that place where time lay suspended, where fancy and legerdemain reside.

And then it came to her, the knowledge that she had been given far more than had been taken away. For a moment, or for as long as she cared to keep her, there really did exist a lovely lady in green.

Chapter Nine

"I'm rather a splendid creature, actually. I wonder why he didn't see that?" Effie's nose ran. Ramona cringed at the sight of so much liquid emanating from her friend. She got up and walked to her bathroom for a tissue. Returning, she handed a blue one to Effie.

"For God's sake, woman, stop sniveling and blow your nose."

Effie obeyed. Ramona jumped at the clear-toned honk. "How such a wonderful woman can indulge in outright sentimentalism is beyond me. He wasn't worth it. Forget him."

Tears surfaced in Effie's grey eyes, threatening to topple onto the path first scouted by others a good ten minutes before. She honked again.

Ramona surrendered. "All right. I'm sorry I said anything. Forget it."

Effie shook her head. Thick dark curls danced round her small face.

"No, you're right, of course, as usual. I never should have trusted him. His eyes are too close together."

Ramona sighed. She had just spent what now appeared as wasted time explaining the modus operandi of an emotionally-distant man to her friend, who apparently, was not listening.

Effie moaned. "If I had had a wisdom figure, she could have warned me. Her sage advice would have been, 'Never trust a man whose eyes are too close together.'"

"Oh, for God's sake, Effie."

"You already said that. As soon as I'm finished crying, I'm going to call the girls and advise *them*. After all, what are mothers for if not a sort of clearing house for experiential grief?" She blew her nose again, taking note for the first time of the now wadded tissue. "You should never buy dyed paper products, Ramona. They can be very dangerous. The dyes pollute, besides which they can cause bladder infections..."

"Pardon me."

"You don't have to be sarcastic. I was just sharing with you."

"You were bleeding all over my rug, my freshly-washed dog, and then you have the audacity to question the color of the band-aid I offer."

"I see your point. You offer much more than band-aids, friend. You offer sage advice. Just like a mother."

"Thank you." Ramona's wide-bodied charm filled the room.

"Do you really think he's a jackass?"

"I didn't say jackass. I said a clod and a churl."

Effie sniffed. "Which translates to...?"

"All right. Jackass."

"Tell me again what a jerk he is."

"He's a jerk."

"Say it with feeling."

"Effie, it doesn't make any difference whether he's a jerk or not if there's chemistry involved. That's the whole sad point. However, why you chose to love such an inappropriate one is beyond me."

"Because, damn it, I didn't know he was inappropriate!"

"He wasn't there for you like he said he'd be. That's pretty inappropriate."

"I hoped, I really thought that after reading my letter, he'd leave his warm nest once and for all, knock on my door, pull me into his arms and make mad passionate love to me."

"How can you expect him to come knocking on your door when he's terrified to knock on his own?" Ramona rapped her knuckles on the wood burl coffee table. "Knock, knock, nobody home."

Effie glared at her. "Now that was cruel."

"Now I'm starting to lose patience with you. I'm starting to get angry. You are a victim of the false romanticism so inculcated into us through film and television. Women are especially vulnerable. We tend to believe that garbage about clothes melting away as the light of day dissolves into darkness. You want to make love on the beach like Deborah Kerr and Burt Lancaster? You know what happens when you make love on the beach? You get sand up your crotch, that's what happens!"

"Oh, shut up."

"I'm just trying to understand all this. I'm trying to be your friend. Perhaps it's time you explained exactly what the attraction was."

"He knew about flowers."

Ramona's eyes widened. "That's it? He knew about flowers? That's a terrific reason for falling in love. With a florist. With a gardener."

"Don't be sarcastic."

"I'm not, damn it! I'm trying to make you see how ridiculous this is."

"It wasn't only flowers," Effie continued. "It was poetry too. He quoted Browning and Sarton and Hopkins. 'As kingfishers catch fire, as dragonflies draw flame.' And *Winnie the Pooh*. He used to recite *Winnie the Pooh* to me."

"That's just great, if you're four. And think about it. A hundred thousand other English majors know all that stuff. You plan on hopping into bed with all of them?"

"Only the ones who touch my soul."

"With what? Pretty words? Sounds to me as if all you got were pretty words. It's not enough, Effie."

"I know that. But I had the hope of something more: the *possibility*."

"Ah, now I see."

"See what?"

"What this is all about. Giving up the dream of something grand. The real flesh-and-blood man wasn't there for you, the flawed, frail human being."

"I wanted him to be. I love all of him, his craggy face, his grey thinning hair, his golden cock. 'It's all yours,' he said. Boy, what a farce."

Ramona raised one eyebrow, giving Effie a cynical look. "He said my golden cock is yours? Jesus, what an arrogant prick!"

"Golden is my adjective and he said it in the heat of passion, but yes, he did say it."

"Well, there's the solution then. Hold him to his word. Separate the man from the myth."

"Ramona, you are unbelievable."

"I'm just trying to get you to see how ludicrous all this moaning is. All this pain."

Effie shrank back. "It's my pain and I'm entitled to it."

"Just don't get lost in it, sweetie. Don't be gobbled up by the sweet sadness of it all. You are not the tormented, rejected lover forever destined to roam the sacred hills alone. The existential heroine lost in the cavernous depths of her own misery."

"I like walking alone. It puts me in touch with the earth. Oh god, Ramona! When I think of all the time I spent with him in independent study. All along he was getting *paid* to seduce me!" Ramona's Old English Sheepdog, Chaucer, came over and sat down on Effie's foot. She hugged him and entwined her fingers in the dog's thick coat.

"Write about it. Write about how compartmentalized he is, how compartmentalized many men are. Write about how disconnected he is. Crucify him if it makes you feel better."

"I can't crucify him. He's Jewish."

Ramona's brow furrowed in confusion. "So was Jesus," she answered.

"I'm not in the mood for comparisons, Ramona. And I don't want to carve him into bits and pieces, even with words. I'm not coming from a place of revenge or bitterness."

"Well then, honor the love you felt. Honor the feelings. And then, for gawd's sake, recognize that you have become obsessed."

"The thing that first attracted me to him was the talk of risking, of the importance of living a life open and vulnerable to all that presents itself, all that comes your way."

"There's little risk in talking a good game."

"I can see that now."

Ramona's voice was gentle. "Maybe that was the problem. You were a grand attraction and a grand repellent at the same time."

Effie's eyes registered confusion. "What do you mean?"

"I mean for him to acknowledge what you were all about, *your* willingness to risk, to live on the edge, was to acknowledge his own failure. You are a constant reminder of that. You'll notice he didn't leave his comforts. But you are ahead of the game. You know what he doesn't."

"Clue me in. Which is?"

"That living on the edge is the only place to live."

"Ramona, I grabbed his hand and jumped, loving the free fall. It wasn't until much later that I looked around and realized the goddamn bastard was wearing a parachute. The landing aches."

"So write about the failure, the weakness. Write about the real man. As much as you saw, as much as you were allowed to see. Write about his strengths too. Honor the best in both of you."

Sorrow lined Effie's face. "He said he wanted to write like a woman. And I bought into that, fell for the subtext of those fine words."

"He can't write like a woman. He doesn't know how. But you do. Only a woman can write like a woman. As the song says, 'Only Women Bleed.'"

"I wish I could stop bleeding," Effie replied. "Much more of this and they'll be treating me for iron-deficiency anemia." She sniffed again.

"Go wash your face and we'll go out. You'll feel better."

"I don't have any money to go out. And you always treat."

Ramona looked at her watch. "We can go to happy hour at the Cantina, have a margarita. They'll feed us for nothing, just hors d'oeuvres, but who cares?"

"I don't know," Effie said. "What if some lounge lizards try to pick us up?"

"And what if they don't?"

Ramona noted the unhappiness on Effie's pixie face.

"Oh, god, Ramona. Some days I feel so old."

Chapter Ten

How you misunderstood him! You assumed that the act of sex would draw you together—would be the grand secret that allowed access. You had imagined locking eyes across a room and he would know you were thinking about how it felt to intertwine your legs with his. How was he supposed to know this? You were convinced he would simply *know*, though not of course in any rational sense. No explanation was needed; it was the wonder of your love. You would breathe life into the relationship, as you had once breathed psychic air into a balding tire, praying your efforts would see you safely home. What a child you were, with an adolescent's romantic vision of love! What you had not understood was how, for a man such as Walter, naked was frightening business. Sex was a risk, an opening up. Your sexual embrace was scary because of the emotional connection it symbolized.

You wonder where your naïve belief that a man could make everything right originated. Why had you been so willing to believe his every word? One reason had to do with the fact that you try always to be honest in your relationships with others. You had no reason to believe that for some, things are not as simple. Another question looms ever present, unanswered. Why had you needed to believe? Ramona was correct; you are obsessed.

With Julie's help, Effie began to see the situation was hopeless, had been hopeless from the beginning. "Sometimes, Julie, he would become angry with me, usually over something I wrote. Only I never knew *what,* exactly, I had written to incur his wrath. Instead of talking about it, he'd withdraw. Bewildered, I'd pick up the phone and he'd hang up on me."

"What did you do?"

"I'd call back."

Julie nodded.

"One night I called back four times. 'I don't know why you're so hurt, so angry,' I said to him. And I really didn't know. 'You know,' he said. But I didn't. And to continue to prod made me feel stupid. Was I supposed to be a mind reader? I saw so very little of him that my letters were the primary means of communication, and sometimes I expressed my disappointment, usually because he had canceled plans, or broken a date."

"You were hurt."

"Yes, and I told him so."

"Do you think he took this as criticism? Could he have seen you as a powerful, angry woman?" Effie thought about this. "It appears as though he didn't want you to feel hurt and he didn't want to feel responsible for that hurt, and then he didn't want to talk about it. Does that sound right?"

"Yes. And then he'd assign blame to me. Everything was my fault—for not understanding, for being hurt, for expressing my feelings."

"It's difficult to communicate with someone who perceives everything you say as an attack, Effie."

"I see that now. I think he took all my confrontations as personal assaults. And then he'd counterattack. It was always my fault for not understanding. And I tried so hard to understand, Julie."

Julie sat silent for a time. "Often, in cases such as this, I work with a client on *how* to communicate. But I don't think his response has much to do with you. It sounds as though he just wanted to be in control. He wanted things his way. As most of us want things our way. What we need to work on is why you found this guy so attractive in the first place."

"I know. But why wouldn't he talk to me about issues between us?"

"Who knows? Oftentimes people who are not interested in hashing out difficulties are protecting themselves from any responsibility they have for the failure of a relationship. It's much easier to assign character deficiencies to another than it is to take a hard, painful look at oneself."

Effie rearranged herself on the sofa. "What hurt the most was being in pain and not being able to discuss it."

"It sounds as though he was not concerned with your pain and he most certainly didn't want to think he had anything to do with your feeling that way."

"He wrote me a letter once in which he claimed I had won a Pyrrhic victory. For what, I never knew. He accused me of solipsism, of sophistry, which is pretty funny coming from the academic."

Julie shook her head. "Can you see how hopeless this was for you? Can you see what a power struggle you two engaged in? What did you do about his letter?"

"I cried. I raged. Finally I called him up and apologized for hurting him, even though I didn't know *how* I had done such a thing."

"Did he apologize?"

"No."

"How would you like to spend the rest of your life apologizing, never knowing why? It doesn't sound to me as though you were in a relationship at all. Can we look at that matter and try to see why? Let's explore your obsession with this man."

Effie said nothing.

Julie continued. "His hanging up on you, his refusal to talk except on his terms. What do you think that indicates?"

Effie shrugged. "Probably that he's not a very nice man."

Julie nodded, then continued, "Over time people become alienated from their spirituality and their creativity whenever they let controlling attitudes predominate."

"And yet he told me he was on a spiritual quest."

"Sounds as though he talks a good game. What are you feeling right now?"

"Hurt. Anger. Mostly hurt. He said he loved me."

"The man may have said he loved you, but do you think he acted as though he did?"

"No. But because he didn't want to or because he didn't know how?"

Julie shrugged. "What difference does it make? Your job isn't to change him or to wish he behaved differently than he did. And now, with hindsight, can you see the signs you were given from the start? If so, next time, you'll be able to recognize them sooner and figure out why a man like that is so intriguing to you so that it never happens again."

"I didn't know he was like that. Not at first."

"Most of us have a family member or two or friends who behave poorly. They are never what they seem at first. But now you do know what he's like. The question for you is, with what you know now, will that help inform your choices going forward?"

ᏮᏮᏮᏮ

After a week of silence, Effie picked up the phone. The mistake she made was not phoning Julie. "Walter, we need to talk. If you hang up on me, then I shall talk to you in dreams. I can do that, you know."

He chuckled. "I'll require proof. You'll say you visited and I'll say no, you didn't, and you'll say yes, I did. You just don't remember."

"Do you think it was my capacity for imagining that got us into trouble?" she asked.

"Yes."

"But you allowed me to."

Walter sighed. "You always have to have the last word, don't you? You always have to be right."

Effie thought about this statement. "Your spiritual advisor might say all that came from you."

"Yes. He probably would say that."

"Whether one talks to deer or one talks to people, it's all the same, don't you think?"

"I imagine."

"Do you think it was accidental that this witch came into your life?"

"No."

"That's something, I suppose. Have lunch with me."

"I can't."

"Yes, you can. Tuesday. Twelve thirty. I want to talk to you."

"You're being a nag, Effie."

"No, I'm not. I'm a thoroughbred. And I become unbridled with denigrating terminology designed to put me in my place."

"Goodbye," he said quickly, the lilt of glibness catching in his voice.

"See you Tuesday," she said, listening as the hum of the dead line droned in her ear.

ৡৡৡৡ

The day before their planned lunch, Walter called and left a message on her answering machine that he couldn't make it. Some hurts exist beyond time. She was unwilling to admit that he had taken her words to heart, had already and so easily put their brief relationship behind him. And then came his missive. "Let it go," he wrote, "and the pain will go too."

What a bastard he was, using women to his own end! To hell if she'd let it go on his time frame; she'd let it go when she was damn good and ready.

She thought back over their time together, recognized that she had been the one who had given so freely of herself. Walter had fit her into his over-programmed schedule when he could, had thought nothing of canceling dates if something better came along. She knew he would have argued he spent valuable time writing her letters. Big of him. But Effie as writer knew that what was written was as much for the author as for the recipient. The picture he painted of himself was just the one he wanted her to receive. He hid behind financial worries, which she knew were real enough but were also another convenient block to intimacy.

"Is this catch what we can catch when we can catch it?" she once asked him.

"I'm afraid so, but not necessarily because I want it that way."

If Effie had wanted something different, she would have worked to change it. How had she, in a few short months, gone from the one bright spot in his life, to his major discomfort? She had read recently in a self-help book that some men don't like women who are as smart as they are. They don't want to spar with women; they don't want to be challenged. They come to women for their feminine attributes, which sounded to Effie suspiciously like Marabel Morgan's *The Total Woman*. Only the woman Morgan presented was not total: She was an airhead in see-through lingerie, high heels and an apron. With her mouth pasted shut. With her writing arm cut off.

ૐ ૐ ૐ

Walter had once written to her that as a child he had flung bottles out to sea, bottles containing notes he hoped would be found by Admiral Byrd or Eleanor Roosevelt or Albert Einstein or Gene Autry. His fantasy was that these people would share their secrets with him.

The story had touched her, reached her on a level that required response. She wrote back to the seven-year-old Walter, the boy she had only glimpses of, the boy who jumped off roofs and read voraciously and wished he were an Indian. And pretending she was Eleanor Roosevelt come unexpectedly upon Walter's childish scrawl filled her with joy unimaginable, allowed her to enter the child's sense and sensibilities. She went beyond wonder, and in doing so, wrote to him:

Dear Walter,
It was with heartfelt surprise that I found and read your note. I understand you like to study about Indians. I like Indians too. You must surely be an imaginative boy whose dreams take him far beyond the sea. I would like to share a

secret with you, a secret that has helped sustain me in difficult times: Hold fast to your dreams. Like notes in a bottle, time dulls our visions, but it is up to us to keep dreams bright, as bright as evening stars in a desert sky. Shine with the intensity of your vision and you shine for others. Poet William Blake might have said it best: "He whose face gives no light shall never become a star." In my book, young man, you are a star.

    Sincerely,
    Eleanor Roosevelt

Effie had written to Walter about growing up without a mother, about the loneliness, and he never once said a word, never acknowledged the pain in her young life. Why then, did she find it so surprising that he was unable to acknowledge her current sorrow?

Chapter Eleven

Effie walked into the office she shared with Francine, another English instructor.

"Oh, I didn't expect to see you here."

"Thought I'd eat lunch in here today," Francine said, "and catch up on some grading."

"It's endless, isn't it? Francine, I have news. Guess what?"

Francine looked at her. "Remember the young man who was in your freshman composition class and when he asked about an instructor for literature, you suggested me? Billy. Billy Schneider, I believe. Anyway, nice kid. Enthusiastic."

"I remember him. Engineering student."

"*Was* an engineering student. Billy told me after class today that after taking your class and now mine, that he was switching majors. He's going to pursue a degree in English."

Francine laughed. "His parents are going to hate us. Kid probably had a good future firmly secured."

"Well, he'll be a terrific professor, if that's what he's aiming for. He's a good writer as well."

"'Nothing so fits a person for a life of dedicated, useless unhappiness, as four years of majoring in English.' Recall that quote? From the *Whole Earth Catalog*, I think."

"And it gets worse. At the very least, add another two years for a master's degree. Look, I have to grab a bite to eat before my next class, but let's sit down sometime soon and really talk."

"I'd love to," Francine responded. "See you soon."

Effie sat on the comfortable leather chair in Julie's home office.

"Julie, I am so miserable."

"Tell me why."

"Because he said I always had to have the last word."

"Is that true?"

Effie sniffed. "Yes, it's true."

"Why do you think it's true?"

"Because as a child I never had the last word." Effie was beginning to see the parallels: She had been loved and adored as a child as long as she kept her mouth shut. "As a kid I could be funny, but if I transgressed, Daddy was right there saying, 'Don't be smart.' What did he want me to be—stupid? Does that sound unconditional?"

Julie looked at her, silently inviting her to elaborate.

"Maybe if I could have learned the art of refraining, he'd still be around. I'm a terrible refrainer."

"From what you've told me, this man is a narcissist. Your relationship was doomed from the start. He didn't want you. He wanted you to reflect his light. Do you think he was telling you he wanted you to love the illusion of him, without question?"

Effie started. "Jesus, Julie, you are more of a witch than I am. I said that very thing to him. 'It was my ability to create you,' I said. I asked him if he thought people chose with whom they fell in love, and he said he recognized that it wasn't an intellectual process, if that's what I meant."

"Can you see how inappropriate he was for you?"

"Yes. On the one hand, all the necessary ingredients for a strong attraction were there. On the other, all those take-charge needs of his fought my own stay-on-top-of-it illusions. When I was just a kid, my dad used to spend Saturday afternoons playing games with me—cards, dominoes, Chinese Checkers. He had such a desire to win that if he found I was ahead, he'd change the rules."

"You're kidding? Most parents go out of their way to let their children win a few."

"I know it sounds funny, and sort of pathetic, but that so-and-so couldn't stand to lose, especially not to a kid, so he rearranged the rules to suit his own needs."

"So you grew up expecting the rules to change?"

"I grew up never knowing *what* to expect. In one respect, nothing surprises me, so I suppose that's healthy. And it has given me a certain flexibility. But it also allowed me to see very early on how upset some people become when you don't play the game their way, how upsetting it is if you don't behave yourself."

"Like your lover?"

Effie nodded, assimilating the comparison. "As I got older, my father let me win a few, probably because he knew I remembered his made-up rules better than he did." She sighed. "If only we understood the rules ahead of time."

"You can see what's going on now, can't you?"

"Yes, but it doesn't make it any easier. I wounded the professor's masculine pride with my insistence on forthrightness, and all along he was trying to tell me to accept him for what he was." Effie knew she didn't want to be right all the time; she just wanted to be *heard*. It was not a desire to be right as much as a primal response to people in positions of power, however illusory. The hair on the back of her neck stood up when confronted with a controlling male. She saw red. She sank her heels in like a six-year-old. "Can't make me," she'd say. "Won't do it." A mid-forties, six-year-old.

"Maybe he wasn't as interested in you accepting him for what he was as much as for what you both wanted him to be."

Walter's passion for writing was one of the qualities she had found so exciting. But a spirit only half soars on broken wings. And she was beginning to suspect that Walter was a man who denied the full limit of himself. "I made no demands of that man. It doesn't make any difference now, anyway. 'It's all illusion,' he said. That goddamn writer!"

"Do you think anyone wants someone else messing with their illusions?"

"I thought the reason men and women came together in the first place was to expand the soul, the imagination. That's all I wanted."

Julie smiled at her, a bit sadly. "Can you see that from a man like that, you asked too much? It sounds as though who you fell in love with—aside from the illusion—was the struggling writer-professor, who continually falls in love with talented lovely student-writers, who promises to be there for them and then as soon as it gets sticky, hides behind the serenity of his wife, his dog, his rose bushes. Is that what you want? A man who takes advantage of his position to woo his female students?"

Effie responded. "You're right. And then he hops right back to his wife, ex-wife, whatever her status is, hops back to his dog and roses. The sea is awash with women who rode out the tsunami of this guy. What a fool I've been!"

"Can you see how leaving James might have made him uncomfortable?"

"Of course. Pressure by example."

"And can you see that no woman is going to change this man?"

"'I can't be what you want,' he said. 'I can't give you what you want.'"

"Try substituting *won't* for *can't*. Isn't that closer to the truth?"

Effie thought about this and nodded.

"Tell me why you called him."

"Because I always have to have the last word."

Julie laughed. "Now, tell me why you really called him."

"Because I wanted to hear his voice. He talked to me for almost twenty minutes."

"Big of him. Is that enough for you?"

"No, it's not. I told him the situation as it stands was not acceptable to me. In the beginning, I told him I was not willing to sacrifice his friendship for something as silly as sex. I guess I did. I wanted to talk to him about it. We planned lunch, or I planned lunch, and then he canceled."

"Were you surprised?"

"No. Hurt. Not surprised. Sometimes I think he misinterprets things on purpose. He decides what I mean and that's that, end of discussion. Talk about having the last word."

"We need to talk about why you were willing to settle for so little."

"I'm looking at that. He was attractive to me because he is brilliant, witty, a lover of illusion. Just like someone else I knew well."

Julie raised her eyebrows. "Do you think you've been yearning for what is unavailable?"

Effie nodded. "I've been so selfish, Julie. So self-absorbed. I've hurt my children, though I have to say they're so busy with their own lives, they don't act hurt. And if his ex-wife knows, I've hurt her as well." Effie thought a moment. "Even if she doesn't know, I've still hurt her." She sniffled.

"So what are you going to do about it?" Julie asked.

"I can apologize to my children and hope they'll forgive me. But her? I don't want to cause her any more pain than my actions already have. I have to change my ways. Can you help me, Julie?"

Julie smiled. "That's what I'm here for."

Even in his absence Walter Rabinowitz taught Effie things. Or because of him, she taught herself. Acknowledging that creation is sparked by compassion, by tenderness, she strived to write with generosity, with freedom, with an awareness of her own truth. And in the act of writing she learned, learned that the reason she was a writer was because it was the one place she could make things turn out the way *she* wanted. She learned that whom we love—and how—is but an unconscious re-enactment of early experience, even though painful. She learned that the pains of her childhood had not been mourned because she had neither the capacity nor the strength to do so. Grief is connected.

She came to see that her losses were inextricably linked to her gains. Whatever we love is easy to write about, though not always easy to understand. Writing was the attempt to understand. She came to see that there existed between herself and Walter Rabinowitz a powerful connection, a connection she was just beginning to understand, and whether he acknowledged it or not was for her a moot point: He acted as listener. (Or more correctly, she had *hoped* he would act as listener.) It was some subterranean notion of hers that by persisting, eventually a clarity would evolve. For now she strolled a modern art museum; the blurbs and splotches were colorful, but none of them made any sense. To feel, must we first see?

In terms of him, she only felt, only saw what she chose to see, had ignored essential warning signals because she wanted so desperately to believe her magic was strong. And now she recognized she must forgive them both: the ultimate act of loving.

The process was bewildering, sometimes sad, sometimes even amusing, as she let her writer's imagination take her places that in real life she might not visit. She was thankful she had words, a place to take the confusion. What did others do, people who had no chapters to hide behind, places in which to lose themselves? (Places in which to find themselves?)

She learned to like being alone because it was easier to live in the *now* alone. Easier to concentrate, to observe. The danger was becoming selfish and self-absorbed. And what good are we as humans if we don't give, don't share? But first we must come to an understanding, an acknowledgment of our most private selves.

Her vision, her viewpoint encompassed and recognized both sides of the dramatist's mask—and related to each. She remembered him saying, "To make it funny you first make it sad." As she recalled so many things he said. And laughing felt better than crying, though always there was the acknowledgment that right below the surface rested…the other.

Some days she was pleased to note a light at the end of the tunnel, but then came the recognition that it was only another goddamn freight train headed her way. It was no wonder she wrote fiction. No wonder.

She noticed Julie watching her, as she watched Julie. "I don't understand where James fits in, Julie. James, who is the antithesis of my father."

"Your mother, perhaps," she explained. "The mother who wasn't there for you. James gets to be the loyal martyred mother who takes care of you, who smothers you while you hurt him. How does that fit?"

"Jesus. Do you know any relationships that aren't based on neurotic needs?"

"A few. A very few."

"I thought people married their opposite parent."

"Usually, but most often we marry the person with whom we have the most issues."

"I guess I do have issues with my mother, especially seeing as how she wasn't even there. You are really helping me to see. Thank you for that."

"That's what I'm here for."

"How did you know he had rose bushes?"

"Men like that always have some source of comfort."

"Hmmn."

"Are you writing?"

"Yes, but it takes enormous faith in one's abilities, especially to create anything of length."

"What about the poetry?"

"The poetry class was helpful because it gave me an immediate outlet for the pain I was feeling rather than having to wait for chapters down the road. But I'm not a poet. My job is not the poet's. My vision is more extended, less pure perhaps. If I burned like that all the time, I'd soon burn out. I prefer to slow cook, to let ideas simmer."

Julie looked at the clock on the table. "We have to stop for today. But don't you stop simmering."

"Simmering's not the problem. It's losing all my juices. I worry about overkill."

"I think not. I suspect you have resources you don't even know about."

"Maybe. If only finding them didn't hurt so much."

They were interrupted by a knock on the door of Julie's home office. "Mom, I need to use the car."

"Not now," Julie said, "I'm with a client."

"But I need it *now!*" came the plaintive cry from the hallway.

"My apologies. I told my family I'd be done and now we've gone a bit over." She got up, went to the door and opened it. "I said, not now, Keith. I'm not finished in here as yet."

Effie could hear the teenager arguing. Ultimately, Julie went to her purse and extracted the keys.

"Thanks," Effie heard him mumble.

Julie's face, when she turned back to Effie, was non-committal. Effie laughed. "What's so amusing?" Julie asked.

"You."

"Why?"

"Because you have all the expertise and yet when it comes right down to it, where it counts, you're just like the rest of us."

"Geesh! Teenagers. And I apologize again for the intrusion. This is the downside of a home office."

Effie laughed again. "I know. They know just what buttons to push, don't they?"

"Yes. The mother buttons."

Effie stood up. "See you next week, Mom." The two women smiled at each other. "I'm so glad to know you're a human being underneath all that professionalism, Julie. But then, I suspected that."

"My humanity is part of the work I do with you, Effie, with all my clients."

Effie nodded. "See you next week, then."

Chapter Twelve

All three women glowered at the guilty party. "Exactly what was the meaning of your bringing a man to our meeting?" Blythe glared at Lucy.

Lucy bit her lower lip and looked as though she might cry.

"You know the rules," Ramona admonished. "No visitors."

"But I didn't think...I mean...He's a serious writer. He's published."

"We can see that you didn't think," Ramona continued. "The one rule is, and we decided this together, is that the group consists of just the four of us. We have something precious here and we need to preserve it."

"Did you notice yourself waiting on him, Effie?" Blythe studied her friend.

"I did not wait on him."

"You did too. I saw you. You asked, 'What would you like in your coffee, Dan?' You never ask me what *I* want in my coffee. You make me get it myself."

"Which is just what I did with him," Effie countered. "I'll admit I *started* to serve him, but I caught myself. And I don't *make* you get anything, Blythe. I leave all the goodies on the kitchen counter so each person can serve herself, just like everyone else does." Effie looked at Lucy. "Because you brought Dan, Lucy, now Blythe thinks I engage in preferential treatment."

"I had a funny piece to read about my visit to the gynecologist," Blythe said. "How was I supposed to read that in front of him?"

Ramona looked at her curiously.

"It was my normal yearly visit, okay?" Blythe stared her down.

Lucy sniffed and blinked back tears. "I only invited him because we became friendly in my writing class, and he

asked if I knew of any groups he could join and so I...well..."
Three sets of unsympathetic eyes stared at her.

"There's a certain immediate visceral response that occurs between women reading their work, which is very precious, Lucy." Ramona continued. "Either we maintain the intimacy of the group or we do not."

"You mean we maintain the exclusivity," Lucy snapped.

"Call it what you will," Blythe responded.

"I had a chapter I wanted to read about the big jerk in my life," Effie said. "Only I couldn't because in talking to Dan I realized he might very well know him. This is a small world, Lucy, and we are saying to you that we think you have taken away the feeling of safety we've always had amongst us. I cherish that."

"Me too," Blythe said.

"Me three," Ramona said.

"I'm sorry. It won't happen again. So what do you want me to tell him when he asks about our next meeting?"

"Tell him we quit for the summer," Blythe suggested.

"But it's only May."

"Tell him we quit for May."

"God, Lucy," Ramona intoned. "How could you have done such a thing? I feel so invaded."

"Me too," Blythe agreed. "Although he was sort of cute."

"You see?" Effie said. "You would have waited on him as well."

"Would not."

"Would too."

"Would not."

"Ladies," Ramona warned. "You see what happens, Lucy? No visitors."

δ❧δ❧δ❧

Edward Hines, screenwriter and Walter's occasional writing partner, lived in a wood-and-glass apartment complex on one of Malibu's funkier beaches. Attractive, expensive homes sat next to dilapidated, expensive shacks. Effie and Walter had several times enjoyed a dinner at Edward's home.

When Effie arrived for a visit on a Sunday afternoon, Edward welcomed her. "Effie, come in. I was just sitting down to work."

He led the way into the interior of the apartment, decorated in shiny chrome and glass. Everything was impeccably neat, so neat it made Effie uncomfortable. What did Walter think of all this, she wondered? Walter, who was disorganized and messy. She had noted earlier that a messy office was symptomatic of a messy-minded person, perhaps even an emotionally- confused person. At least her theory held true for Walter. Why hadn't she paid attention to this information? Why hadn't she integrated it into some sort of cohesive picture of the man before becoming involved?

"A cup of tea?"

"Yes, thank you, if you're having one."

"Thank you for your note."

Effie looked at him. "To be perfectly honest, Edward, my motives weren't one hundred percent pure. But I guess you knew that."

He smiled. "I suspected as much."

"Maybe they were sixty-five percent pure." She gazed out the sliding glass door to the sea beyond. "Nice view." Pelicans flew in formation against the skyline. Pink clouds studded an otherwise clear sky.

Edward handed her a cup of tea. "How goes it with you and Walter?"

"It doesn't, Edward. That's why I'm here. Walter wants to call it quits and we never even got started."

"Hmmn. Did he say why?"

"I called it quits but I really didn't want it to be over. I just wanted to quit hurting. He didn't have to agree with me. Now he wants me out of his life. He said that the relationship reminded him of a sweater he had desperately wanted in junior high school—a sweater he worked his butt off for, but when he finally got it home, it scratched."

"Ah, the old sweater story."

"Where it gets scratchy is where it gets interesting. He thinks you throw love away, trade it in for a new design the moment things get rough."

"And you're hurting."

"Hurting? I feel as though someone yanked out my heart, did a tap dance on it and then split for Argentina. Someone with big feet."

Edward nodded. "Let it go, Effie. You'll find it doesn't change anything. Not really. Find yourself a plumber."

"A plumber? What is that supposed to mean?"

Edward took a drink of his tea and leaned forward. "Do you want to write or do you want to fuck?"

"What does that mean, Edward? Are you propositioning me?"

"What I meant was that you are going to have to squelch the woman in order to write."

Effie could feel her cheeks redden. "Excuse me? Squelch the woman? Might as well say, 'squelch the source.' No one said to Bach or Picasso or Mozart, 'Choose between your art and your fulfillment as a man.' Men, I've noticed, manage to write and to fuck, though perhaps not successfully if one takes into account their fragmented, disjointed view of themselves and the universe." Effie took a deep breath to avoid hyperventilating. "It's the age-old patriarchal warning, isn't it, Edward? 'Woman, this is man's territory, and if you choose to tag along, unsex yourself.' To hell if I will."

Edward ignored her outburst. "Have you met Walter's mother?"

"No."

"She's an interesting woman. Strong. I think he has problems with his mother."

"Terrific. Shall we blame good ol' mom?"

Edward took another drink of tea. "When the woman before you said goodbye, I think he was taken by surprise, the effect of which was to make him shut down even further."

"She surprised him? Did he expect her to wait around forever? She told him she was marrying someone else and he had no idea there even *was* a someone else." Effie fondled her teacup, felt the warmth against her hand. "At least it's not just me he treats this way, if that's any consolation." When she looked up, Edward was watching her.

"Effie, let it go. The man is nuts."

"Everyone is nuts close up, Edward."

"He's ephemeral as smoke."

"So I've discovered. 'I'll be there,' he said. 'Either way.'"

"He said that? He meant it then."

"'You are magical,' he said."

"Effie, the man is a poet, a mad poet. Be thankful you two didn't end up in a condo somewhere. You would have killed each other."

"Why do you say that?"

"Because you are as neurotic as he is."

"Neurotic? Neurotic is becoming best friends with the man who cuckolded you, Edward, who took away your woman."

"Ouch. How did you know?"

"He told me. Bragging, I guess. Or apologizing."

"He's very controlling."

"No kidding."

"Effie, he needs a woman like I have now: accepting, uncomplicated, undemanding."

Fury burned in Effie's brain. "You don't want a woman, Edward, you want a Bassett Hound—a mute, adoring mutt who will fetch your slippers, who will be there when you want her to be, no questions asked. What about relationships that require our deepest, secret selves?" She stood up to leave. "Thank you for the talk. I'm beginning to see now how loving me was for Walter a dreadful pain in the ass." She looked into Edward's eyes. "I was the best thing that ever happened to that man."

"Effie, they were *all* the best thing to happen to him. If it gives you any comfort, he's a moral person, an ethical man."

"Using people for your own purposes, Edward, discarding them when they no longer fit the illusion, is not moral."

Edward shrugged. "I'm sorry. Sorry you're hurting. I mean that." He came over, put his arms around her and gave her a hug. Tears threatened to ride down her cheeks.

"I wanted to share with him the magic, Edward. I wanted him to be consumed by the experiences we shared."

Edward nodded. "Let it go, Effie."

ɛ♦ɛ♦ɛ♦

Her conversation with Edward left her sad and confused. Had Walter wanted her to love the *real* man or merely the image? The fantasy or the reality? Real people in real relationships often scratched each other, because in the desire to know, they occasionally poked at exposed nerves, *not* to hurt or to point out weakness, but to love the real person. She realized, of course, that there were relationships where people did indeed set out to hurt the other, but that was not the relationship she desired. Did Walter think he had never harmed her?

Effie understood that he had become his own jailer, that all of us are the authors of our own lives, not just the scripts we write. The key rested in Walter's pocket. Even knowing this, still she had considered him worth the chance. She hadn't asked him to neglect his work. "Commit first to the words on the page," she had told him. She had simply wanted to be there for him, to love him as unconditionally as she could. But she counted as well. And as soon as she stated her desires and needs, he was gone. Vamoosed. Adios, Amiga. Had he thought she was bartering love? She wasn't; she said she'd love him anyway. Would he have wanted a woman who wasn't willing to fight for all she deserved? Was she supposed to have been an ascetic, a Mother Teresa? She had wanted to feel his body next to hers more often than she got. She had wanted to kiss his craggy face, to feel his mouth on her mouth.

Effie was starting to see that the reality about that kind of intimacy was that it had the potential for challenging his fragmentary view of the universe, because for an instant, at least, the *it* Walter claimed he was searching for was removed from consciousness. Perhaps that had been what frightened him off. The post-orgasmic state can tell us who we are; attitudes become the body, the body is spirituality, the *it* we already possess. And Walter was terrified of that. He needed, always, to conduct the search outside of himself.

He had told her he loved her responsibly; Effie could see now that his definition of the word differed from hers. His glibness and his unwillingness to dialogue hurt her deeply. How was she supposed to define terms with someone who was not there?

He had wanted her to accept only his strengths, and when she didn't, he threw her love away. She ached. And scratchy was not an adequate reason; fear was not an adequate reason. Nor was the discomfort he claimed he felt. Never before had she experienced the desire to hit someone, to pummel his chest with her fists. She had wanted a man who recognized the fragile inter-connectedness of all things, who understood the witch who talked to rocks. Why the one person she thought came closest to understanding suddenly and so painfully prevented her from speaking of these things was a hurt she did not comprehend.

So, at last she realized she was unable to reach him. She knew she should stop trying. What was she really forsaking? Not Walter, who had never really been there, but rather her unswerving belief in the possible, which was now severely tested. Giving up the real Walter had been hard enough: Giving up the hope was something so onerous and painful that she found herself clinging like a bulldog, shaking the hell out of things, searching for...?

She had wanted to give him the very best of her, the magical mystery tours. The journeys. For Walter, the price of the ticket had simply been too high.

People had to learn to trust each other, for in that came the attitude of discovery. She could have defended herself against him; instead she chose to make herself vulnerable. And Walter's reticence had cheated them both. He had deprived them of the greatest gift: the brass ring one reached for from the carousel horse. Effie had been willing. Effie had reached, yet all the while she reached alone.

Chapter Thirteen

A very large spider lives in the eucalyptus tree next to the trailer. He—Effie is convinced of the spider's sex—is brown and bulbous. The night they meet she is afraid, though a grudging admiration develops as she watches him repair the web she walked into, not seeing. But do male spiders spin webs? The spider sits high in one corner of his creation and surveys the damage, hesitates but a moment, then moves down the web to begin again the work at hand. It glides purposefully on tenuous threads and Effie thinks, hell, it's all so tenuous.

She recalls the phone conversation when she said she just wanted to sit on the floor and cry with him and he said, "That's your program," and she felt an ache in her belly the size of Kansas, so Effie said something, she can't remember what exactly, and he responded, "You might try reading manifestos on church doors." She realizes now that when he said he needed her, it was only the edge of needing.

She convinces herself that art and bitterness walk hand in hand. She plots her revenge; she will publish stories about him in the literary quarterlies he reads.

More than anything she wishes he would call and say he had reconsidered so she could tell him to fuck off. The difficulty with a rich fantasy life is that it rarely translates into anything fine when shared.

Effie admires a scene from Tom McGuane's *Panama*, where the protagonist nails himself to the front door of his girlfriend's house. Masochism aside, the effect appeals to her, for she is someone who is always on the lookout for memorable visuals. Blood and guts are out, but perhaps she could staple her best dress—with her in it—to the front seat of his car. Her best dress cost over three hundred dollars and is a slinky white number he never saw because he is a cheap son of a bitch and never took her any place nice. Effie nixes the staple routine; he isn't worth ruining a dress that looks wonderful on her, and to proceed with the act in blue jeans reflects no sense of style or aesthetics.

In blue jeans, however, she could sit in the apple tree next to his house and pelt him with the fruit of truth whenever he stepped outside. No doubt she'd only see Ruth, his ex-wife, emerge to take out the garbage and to water the plants. The damn prick can't even take out his own garbage, or worse, he takes it out forty percent of the time and considers himself liberated. He is tricky like that—clever enough to think he is pulling something off. A rotten apple is what she plans to use. Worm infested. The difficulty is, there are not enough maggoty apples in the entire Western Hemisphere to make her feel better.

Right now, Effie considers hatred a purer emotion than love because it shines clean and white for her and she has no difficulty identifying it. Love, on the other hand, is often confused with feelings of warmth, passion and lust. She vows never again to be confused. If necessary she will sit— metaphorically at least—forever waiting for the chance to strike; she is now the viper hidden in the vine, the nut case clinging to the satisfaction of just one well-placed apple splat. Yes sir, she enjoys the visual of him dripping cider, though not on the shirt she gave him.

In her mental picture he is on his way somewhere fine, and after he wipes the sticky stuff from his brow, he begs her to climb down out of his tree. "Get down from there right now!" he admonishes.

"Make me," she says.

"Get down!" he repeats. "Ruth might see you. I'm calling the police."

"And telling them what, Walter? That there's a woman sitting in the apple tree next to your house? That your ex-lover is perched in your tree and she's armed with a deadly McIntosh?"

"Granny Smith," he corrects. "The McIntosh doesn't do well in Southern California. It's not cold enough. You should know that."

"Now who always has to be right?" she answers.

She also says, "Fuck off." Effie is wearing her best white dress and she looks divine and when he emerges from his house he tells her he's reconsidered, at which time she announces, "The book I wrote about you has just sold for a great deal of money and I'm going on a publicity tour and thousands of women the world over will soon know just what a schmuck you are, and I'm here to share half my advance with Ruth because she deserves it after putting up with you for all these years, and now she'll leave you and you'll be absolutely alone, which is exactly what you deserve, and no, you can't keep the dog. You don't even get visitation rights."

The fantasy has been indulged and Effie finds it richly rewarding. For a time.

❧ ❧ ❧

The spider is there working, always working. She admires the creature's dull persistence, even as she flinches to see a moth caught in the translucent snare. She turns the porch light off and tries very hard not to think about it.

Ramona lived in an old house, a cabin really, that had been in her family for several generations. The story Ramona told, apocryphal perhaps, was that at one time the cabin had belonged to a bootlegger during Prohibition, and that he smuggled booze from the valley through the canyon to the beach below. Whether it was true or not, Ramona didn't know, though during a remodel, she and her then-husband had found old whisky bottles littering the area under the house.

Effie drove the winding canyon road, enjoying the scent of ceanothus and sage that drifted through her open windows. New homes were appearing on the hillsides, as developers had discovered they could build in the canyons beyond the three-mile Coastal Commission limitation. Effie knew the development of the area Ramona had known and wandered as a child drove Ramona insane; she was constantly calling the county, creating petitions, going to meetings to do her part to try to save what once was wilderness.

A deer crossed the road in front of Effie. She slowed and waited for it to pass. Down the hill it bounded, disappearing into the chaparral. As she rounded a corner Effie noted the sun glistening off the waters of the Pacific, far below. No wonder Ramona was an artist! Every view was more amazing than the next.

"The thing is, Ramona, I like to think of myself as benevolent, as behaving in a loving, forgiving manner toward my fellow passengers on the planet. I want to open my heart and recognize the essential alikeness of all mankind, but when it comes to Walter, my humanity is shot to hell."

Ramona had a smudge of red watercolor on her nose. "Does most of humanity act in a benevolent manner toward you? I'm not convinced that most people are benign, Effie. Most are out for their own interests first and foremost." She washed a magenta hue through her desert sunset.

"I like your painting."

Ramona looked at her, incredulous. "How can you like this painting? I think it's lousy. It's not finished and I don't know if it will ever be finished. The colors are all wrong. I'm trying to paint the desert and I'm looking at the ocean. I'm struggling to get it right and you waltz in here all abundance and beauty, trying to make me feel good, but the effect is just the opposite because I know you're just trying to make me feel good."

"Geesh! But I really *do* like it, even if it isn't finished. I could no more do what you do than I could fly an airplane. Do you want me to lie and say I think it's yucky? What good would that do?"

Effie gazed out the window to the sea. "Looking at the ocean today, Ramona, reminded me of all the early mornings I took Timmy to the beach so he could surf before school. He'd surf and I'd run on the beach. In those days I rarely passed other runners, at least not that early. I asked Timmy once if he'd teach me to surf. 'I can't do that,' he responded. 'Why not?' I asked him. 'Because I can't be seen in the water with my mother.' 'Who's going to see me?' I said. 'Most of the time I'll be underwater.'"

Ramona laughed. "Do you miss him?"

"I do. But he's not little Timmy anymore. Now he's Tim. He and Angie are happy in Colorado; apparently he enjoys grad school, and she's happy working at a job she loves. Where do the years go, Ramona?"

"I don't know, friend. I don't know. Be quiet now," Ramona said. "I have to concentrate on the sky." She studied the photograph in front of her.

Effie always liked what Ramona considered her "failures." For Effie, it was hard to cast a jaundiced eye on anything Ramona created.

"I really appreciate what you're attempting with that one," she would say, regarding a work in progress, and Ramona would counter with arguments concerning depth and perspective and whatever it was she as artist was attempting, and through it all, they remained fast friends.

Was Effie guilty of a lack of awareness? This struck her as a terrible excuse, an insufficient reason for letting herself off the hook. Behavior which had once appeared as innocuous now came into clearer focus.

Once when she and James were riding up the hill, moving a small bookcase to the trailer, they rounded a curve and spotted a bird hopping around a much smaller bird, peeping. Effie immediately recognized the situation—the smaller bird had fallen from the nest but had not yet mastered the complexities of flight. The larger bird hovered protectively, chirping directions. She and James stopped to watch. "Should we move them?" She asked. They deliberated, James taking the position that the bird might die of fright when confronted by humans, or that touching the baby might dissuade the older bird from further protective action. Effie argued that she thought it was mammals that reacted negatively to human interference. While they discussed the situation, a man in a Porsche, a neighbor of Effie's, came zipping around the corner, narrowly missing the feathered pair.

"There, you see?" she said. "Bird smushers all over the place." It was the difference between looking and seeing, and one was not excused from error because one was not aware, at least not to her way of thinking.

Effie lived in a world of the unaware. Bird smushers all over the place.

To satisfy her conscience, she lifted the baby bird out of harm's way and perched it on a low-lying branch, while the mother bird watched and then flew closer to her charge.

"You know what your difficulty is?" Ramona said. "You can't stand that you made a poor choice. It's damaging to your ego or something. So you get involved in all these circumlocutions, behaviors to try to prove otherwise. Only of course they don't. They only validate that Walter is a bigger jerk than you ever imagined." Ramona blotted her watercolor painting with a sponge.

"You're right," Effie answered. "I can't stand that I was wrong about him, that I made a poor choice—if indeed I did choose, which is not exactly clear to me. Do you think I would have discovered all this creepy stuff about him if I had stayed with James and just had a lowdown sneaky affair? I couldn't do that."

"Yes, because the tiger doesn't change his stripes. It probably would have taken longer, however, because there would have been passionate, surreptitious meetings to keep you occupied." Ramona studied her painting and added another wash. "Men are hunters, Effie. They want what they think is unattainable. It's the quest again."

"It's enough to make me run away and hide forever."

"Don't do that. Write about him. Make him evil and...what's the word? Swarthy. Evil men are always depicted as swarthy."

"Stereotype," Effie said. "Sometimes the most evil are absolutely ordinary. And that's the scary part. We're programmed to accept evilness in those whose dark side is physically projected. One never considers a man who looks like your Uncle Pete to be capable of atrocity."

"Aren't you overreacting? You are making him sound like the Hillside Strangler."

"That's because I feel psychically strangled. And I don't know what to do about it. You can walk around in a suit of armor, but then you never love. It's all crummy." Effie studied Ramona's latest effort. "I do like your painting."

Ramona studied it as well. "I'm not happy with it."

"I still like it, friend. But I'm beginning to question my taste in everything. Tell you what? If you can't sell it, I'll buy it from you."

Ramona smiled. "Thank you, dear heart. Thank you."

Chapter Fourteen

Effie dreams that a cantankerous man comes to her door and complains that her garden is overflowing into his yard. The vines—the cucumbers, the watermelon, the pumpkins—have not respected property lines and have climbed through the fence. She walks with him to the back of the house to look. Ripe plums hang heavy from the ancient tree. "Everything is producing too much," she says. She smiles and hands the man a sweet purple fruit. He takes it but does not eat. They both stare at her prolific garden creeping through the wire.

"I will gladly share with you," she tells him. The man is cranky and not satisfied with her response.

Effie wakes happy. She feels the abundant harvest within her overflowing, encroaching on cranky men.

ᔧᔤᔧᔤᔧᔤ

"I've been thinking about you, Effie, wondering how you're doing."

"I'm all right, Ramona. I've made up my mind to be all right."

"Good. I knew you would."

"I thought about what you said, about what Walter said and about what Edward said and I'll be damned if I'll let him off the hook so easily."

"What?"

"Just because it's easier for *him*. Just because it's what he *thinks* he wants. What about what I want?"

"Effie, this is crazy."

"So what? The entire world is crazy. How can I let go of something that was never mine to begin with? Might as well ask me to let go of the moon and the stars. I spent all morning cleaning. First I cleaned the trailer, then I wrote him a letter announcing my intentions. I figured he deserved that much."

"Did you mail it?"

"Of course I mailed it. What good is an unsent letter?"

"He's going to be pissed."

"Walter doesn't get pissed like the rest of us. Walter gets vexed. The only other person I ever heard use that word was my grandmother. Where does he get off with his archaic locutions?"

"If you want to know what I think, I think this is a lousy idea."

"Well, I don't want to know what you think. It's too late for that. Do you want to hear my letter, yes or no?"

Ramona sighed. "Do I have a choice?"

"It's a long one."

"I'm not going anywhere. Shoot."

"Just a sec. I have to go get it." Effie put down the receiver and was back in thirty seconds. "'Dearest Bear,' it begins. I call him that because he is so big and cranky. Dearest might be overdoing it, but what the hell. Okay. 'Dearest Bear, it's a terrible responsibility being adored, isn't it?' You think that's a good opening, Ramona? Because it seems to me that it is not only a responsibility but also a terrible waste of time. Adored is easier than love, isn't it?"

"Effie, read. I don't have hours here."

"All right; here goes. *I am so angry with you. Angry that I believed you. Angry that you are telling me to let go and the telling is motivated not by concern for my pain, but rather for your own discomfort should I decide to put in an unexpected appearance at your bakery, your beach, your university. I can show up whenever I darn well feel like it. I can enroll in classes taught by Walter Rabinowitz. Anger is very freeing. So is the recognition that I can do whatever I damn well please. If I want to move to your cozy little community and become a writer in residence, I will. If I want to don my bathing suit and sun myself on your beach while you walk the waterfront (trousers rolled, Prufrock), I will. If I want to attend your annual writer's conference, I will. If I want to write you thirty-page letters, I will.*

I am angry that you would presume to inform me that letting go is not a rational process, ignoring all the while that it was the goose and not the gander who sprinkled fairy dust over the whole proceedings. I bet you wouldn't know where to find fairy dust. (The stuff I found must have been old.) Rational, hah! All I wanted you to be was all you claimed you were, when all along you were only...only what? An academic. That's it; a goddamn cheating academic, who seeks not real relationships with real women but rather simple dalliances with adoring students. And yes, they can write letters, as long as they're of the hero-worshipping variety, but the minute they touch the truth, toss the excess baggage.

"You've already mailed this thing, is that correct?" Ramona interrupted.

"Yes. Don't stop me now; I'm just getting to the good part. Let's see, where was I? Oh, yeah...*I think your behavior has been despicable. You think you can just use people up and then throw them away, like old sweaters? Boy, is that cocky! And the academic decides how and when and if. No arguments, please. The academic controls. Whose class is this? And he decides when the party meets and when the party's over. No discussion. No itches. The M.O. of an authoritarian so-and-so. And that is not loving with conscience and responsibility; it doesn't even come close. So don't tell me when to let go because it's my pain and I'll let go when I damn well please, when I feel like it and not before. 'I'll do it because I want to and not because you tell me to,' said the little girl in the story I loved as a child. I plan on loving you for an exceedingly—keep the adverb—long time, whether or not you approve. Some things are unexplainable; this is one of them. If that makes you exceedingly uncomfortable, too bad. I hope it wakes you up nights: Gawd, Effie is out there somewhere loving me and there's nothing I can do about it. I plan on holding on for at least two hundred and fifty pages, perhaps more. You know why? Because there are other gullible women out there, women who are called masochistic if they suppress their own feelings (in a real desire to make the relationship work), or castrating if they assert themselves. And there are men who view women as nothing more than accommodating receptacles, despite all their fine rhetoric to the contrary. And that "organ of accommodation" as you call it, is just as pleasure seeking as any male part, Buster.*

Adoring students are supposed to be thankful for the attentions of the guru master. Jesus! What happens when the student becomes as proficient as the teacher, when she takes the lessons learned and moves a step beyond? When she becomes uncontrollable. To hell with mature relationships. And you decide the pain tolerance, never mind consulting your partner. And what is the other side of pain, Mr. R?

So watch the sun come up with the dog; see if I care. But don't tell me you can't give me what I want because you never once bothered to ask what that was: never once.

Just you wait, Henry Higgins. Just you wait.

"You actually sent that?"

"Damn right I did."

There was silence on the other end of the line. Finally, Ramona spoke. "Good. Good for you."

"Good for me?"

"Yes. He deserves it. What's the Henry Higgins part all about?"

"It's about war," Effie answered.

"War? What does that mean?"

"Let's just say an invasion of sorts. It's me exacting revenge."

"Effie, are you sure you know what you're doing?"

"I'm making the world a safer place for vulnerable women. I'm proving the axiom that hell hath no fury like a woman scorned."

"Poor Walter."

"Poor Walter, my foot. The man is a menace."

"I can see that. Just the same, poor, poor Walter."

Chapter Fifteen

"I met your mother, Walter." Effie listened to Walter's rapid breathing on the other end of the line. She repeated, "I said I met your mother. She's very nice."

"You stay away from my mother!"

"I'm afraid I'm already committed to drive her to her Mahjong game Wednesday afternoon. It's not out of my way at all. She goes to Mahjong, and I go to my therapist. As it turns out, they are both within a half mile of one another. Isn't that a convenient coincidence?"

The line went dead.

Effie called back. "And on Saturday," she continued, "I'm taking her to the Farmers Market. I haven't been to Farmers Market in years, not since I was a child. They used to have parrots there, and mynah birds, outside the basket shop. Do you remember the birds? I wonder if they're still there."

Walter said nothing and Effie had the distinct feeling he was preparing to hang up again, so she quickly added, "Your mother tells me she's very distressed by the fact that her only son no longer goes to temple. I know you don't believe in all that religious hocus-pocus, but would it really hurt you to attend, just on the high holidays? It would make your mother very happy, and really, it's so little to ask."

The line went dead again.

Effie redialed. "In fact, when I told her I knew very little about the Jewish faith, not being Jewish but rather a Methodist and an uninterested one at that, she volunteered to tell me all about the history of your people. 'Our people' is the phrase she used. So of course I said I was interested. I'm always looking to learn new things. Your mother is really a very lovely lady, Walter. Very lovely. She reminds me of a little apple doll, with her round pink cheeks and all. It's difficult, of course, to see how she raised an incorrigible like you, but truth is stranger than fiction now, isn't it?"

Walter did not respond.

"Oh, you needn't worry that I told her I knew you. I would never let on."

"How," Effie could hear him measuring his words, "how, exactly, did you meet my mother?"

"I confess it wasn't entirely accidental, if that's what you're thinking. I went to her neighborhood, and then I waited until I saw her leave her house and when she came back carrying bags of groceries I volunteered to help her with them, and we sort of struck up a conversation, and one thing led to another. I'm a very easy person to talk to, Walter. I think you look just like your mother, except for the fact that her eyes are farther apart, which indicates, I believe, a more generous nature. If she were *my* mother, I'd certainly think about getting her out of that neighborhood. It's sort of run down around there. Shabby? You know what I mean? It might not even be safe for an old woman."

"My mother has lived in that neighborhood for fifty years! I grew up in that part of town! She likes it there. She has her friends, her temple, her...her..." He was sputtering now.

"You don't have to shout at me. I can hear you just fine. Know where else I took her?"

His voice was weak. "Where?" he asked.

"To the bookie."

Walter groaned.

"She said she wanted to place a bet, something she's been doing for a good thirty years. Did you know about that? At any rate, who am I to deny a seventy-five-year-old woman the right to place a bet?"

"Seventy-eight," he corrected.

"Exactly. 'Serendipity in the fourth race,' I told her. And guess what? The luck of the Irish as they say. We won! So of course a firm bond of friendship has been established between us. Now at least, she'll have money for a few extras, which, if you were a good son, you'd already be providing your dear mother."

"Stay away from my mother, Effie!"

"Can't make me."

"I'm warning you."

"Big fat deal." And *she* hung up on *him*.

ော်ော်ော်

Effie shared with Julie her meeting Walter's mother.

"Do you think that was a wise idea?" Julie asked.

"Probably not. Probably not at all. But I wanted him to know that I'm tough, that he can't just use me, use women."

"And do you think your actions furthered that goal?"

"I don't know, Julie. What I want to know is how he could he just turn love off like that?"

"It's easier for the disconnected to disconnect. You might want to think about if he ever loved you in the first place. His behavior certainly suggests otherwise."

Effie wondered if Walter ever thought of her, if he missed her. "'You are a prism,' he said. But you know something, Julie? He's the one who needs to shine, needs to reflect light. Because it magnifies him. Didn't I magnify him enough?"

"You magnified the truth, Effie. It's time you came to grips with the fact that the man you are describing is interested only in himself."

"I magnified the truth because I loved the truth. I wanted to love the real man, the man who tries. That's all: the man who tries."

"You attempted to love the real man, but it doesn't sound as though he wanted that. I want you to consider something, to take a close look at what went on between you. Some people choose cold—that's what they're called in psychological terms—long-term relationships, because of the emotional distance, the comfort zone. At the same time they feel the need for touch, for closeness, so they go in search. At first the relationships they pick are wonderful: passionate, electric, until that moment of crossover when they recognize that part of them requires distance for comfort. Being loved and needed, really loved, what would that feel like? I suspect you were too much for him, Effie. And it's time we take a look at *why* you chose such a person."

"Perhaps some of my own needs were being met? Needs to nurture. I'm a very good nurturer. With me, flowers grow, children blossom, goats produce gallons of milk, chickens too many eggs, men write terrific novels." She stopped. "Fuck it. I'll write my own."

Julie smiled.

"I used to wonder about his wife, ex-wife, whatever she is, about what kept him there. I imagined her horribly maimed or something. But she's not. She walks the dog Monday, Wednesday, and Friday mornings. Or is it evenings? Can you believe I fell in love with a man who negotiates dog walking? Jesus!"

"He wasn't too willing to negotiate with you."

"That's for sure. And I can see now it was because I meant nothing to him. He's moving right along as though I never happened to him. 'I'm on a path,' he said. But you know what I think? It isn't a path so much as an awful treadmill and he refuses to stop and get off and take a good look at things."

"Number one, it takes courage to stop the treadmill. And number two, and more importantly, that's *his* issue, not yours. You can't make things happen for someone else. He has to want change for himself."

"He'll never want it for himself."

"So now you know."

"So why can't I stop obsessing now that I understand all of this?"

"I suspect that, intellectually, you understand. Integrating information emotionally can take a long time."

"I don't have a long time. Much more of this and they'll be shipping me off to the loony bin."

"What about your family? Your teaching? Your writing? We haven't talked much about those issues."

"I know. Sometimes it's all too much."

"Are you keeping a journal? Sometimes it helps to organize one's thoughts."

"Not consistently. I need to get back to that."

"Our time is up for today, but I have a question for you. What happens on Tuesdays and Thursdays?"

"What?" Effie was confused.

"Tuesdays and Thursdays. With his dog."

Effie pondered the question. "I don't know. The poor thing. She's probably constipated."

Effie entered the market; she had never been there before but it didn't take her long to locate Walter.

"Pretty nice tomatoes, wouldn't you agree? Probably from Mexico, though, this time of year. Make sure you wash them carefully." She smiled up at him, expectantly.

The tomato Walter had selected disintegrated in a sodden mass between his fingers.

"Boy, you sure picked a ripe one." Effie pulled a tissue from the cavernous depths of her bulky purse and handed it to Walter. Seeds and thin, watery juice ran down his wrist and mingled with his shirtsleeve. He took the offered tissue and wiped tomato pulp from his hand.

A woman shopper ogled the soggy tomato remains lying on the display and glared at Walter. He grabbed the handle of his shopping cart and careened madly out of the produce section, almost upsetting a display of pineapples.

Effie trotted after him. "If you twist the top off a pineapple, you don't have to pay for something you can't even eat. How's that for a handy hint?" Walter, saying nothing, plunged his cart down the aisle to dairy products, where he seized a pint of half and half. "You just take hold of the top like this..." Effie demonstrated the fine art of pineapple decapitation, "and presto, it's off. Of course you can keep the top and then plant it, but it takes about two years to get one pineapple, so it's hardly worth the effort, in my opinion."

Walter stopped abruptly and hissed at her. "It takes you over an hour to drive down here. Why are you doing this?"

"Because I *feel* like it," she answered. "Nice market. Ritzy. A lot nicer than the one where your poor mother shops."

Walter resumed his rapid tour of the grocery store, with Effie following doggedly on his heels. She watched him stop in front of the canned soups and deliberate. "You gonna buy *that?*" She peered intently at the ingredients list of the product he selected.

Walter sighed.

"Do you know how much tin and other yucky poisonous stuff goes into every can, Walter? Do you have any idea how much of that nastiness filters through the can into the food, into you? And look at the high sodium content." Her eyes widened. "Too high. Way too high, especially for a man your age."

He threw the can of soup into his cart and moved on down the row to the coffee aisle where he studied the coffee bean selection. Effie watched him deliberate and finally choose an imported French roast. "A man your age would be much better off with chamomile tea, don't you think?" She grabbed a box of tea bags and dumped it into his shopping cart. "No doubt you've heard about the hazardous effects of caffeine. There are over 400 toxins in every cup. But decaffeinated, why, that's almost worse, unless of course you buy water processed. Do you know how they process that stuff?" She pulled a can off the shelf and studied the label. With great disdain she replaced the product. "They use cleaning fluid, Walter, or something very similar."

"I know they use cleaning fluid!" He lowered his voice when he noticed other shoppers staring at him. "Effie," he whispered. "Please. Go home. I am not interested. I don't have the strength for this. I'm tired."

"Of course, you're tired, dear. You're rapidly approaching your twilight years. A man of your age ought to slow down a bit. Enjoy life."

"WILL YOU PLEASE QUIT SAYING A MAN OF MY AGE!"

"I think you need to lower your voice, Walter. People are staring."

Walter furrowed his brow and frowned down at her. "You've got to leave this place, at once." Effie detected a discordant, frantic quality to his voice she had not heard before. "At any moment Ruth might come in here," he explained. "She'll need to remind me to get cat food or some such thing."

"Why, Walter, I didn't know you had a cat. A mean ol' Tom, I bet. Am I right?"

In Walter's glare, Effie saw something that caused her to wonder if he ever became violent.

"For your information, Dr. Rabinowitz, I've already met Ruth. I signed up for her class through university extension. I've been twice already and I must say, it's a heck of a drive. Nonetheless, I think you should know that she's a much better teacher than you, not nearly as stuffy." Effie turned and walked quickly out of the market.

Walter abandoned his cart mid aisle and ran after her into the parking lot. "You *can't* be in Ruth's class!" he sputtered. Effie watched as he took a handkerchief from his back pocket to wipe his brow.

"And why can't I? It's a free country." She unlocked her car door.

"Because you can't, that's why. Because I say you can't!"

Effie slid onto the front seat of her car and rolled down the window. "Don't be ridiculous, Walter. I can do whatever I want." She watched as his face turned various shades of purple. She smiled at him and started the motor. "What's your cat's name?" she asked.

The annual Beach Cities Half Marathon, sponsored by Meals on Wheels, ran from Beach Park up a slight grade to the bike path, where it followed a six-and-a-half-mile course to the turnaround. Effie waited in line for her number, then found a spot on the grass where she could do some stretches before the race. After limbering up, she joined the gathering pack of runners at the starting line.

The crowd was thick and it took her some time to make her way through the throng of people to her target. "Hi," she said.

The starting gun sounded. Walter turned around and missed his send-off. The man behind him cursed. Only partially recovered, Walter's legs moved automatically.

"Great day for a race, don't you agree? I've been running for years. It's second nature to me now." Effie jogged next to him. Walter, in a burst of speed, ran ahead. Effie followed suit, catching him four minutes later. "Boy," she panted, "you're in pretty good shape for a man your age. Did you know that if a woman runs with the same degree of exertion as a man, that she reaches her target heart rate much quicker? Take, for example, the two of us."

"There is no such *thing* as the two of us," Walter grumped.

"If a man and a woman are running side by side," Effie continued, "the man might be within his target heart rate range, while the woman may be exceeding hers. As a consequence, the woman may overexert herself."

"I certainly wouldn't want you to do that." Walter sneered at her and with a renewed burst of energy, ran ahead once more. Effie contemplated him from the rear. He certainly did have cute legs. For a man his age.

"There are other cardiovascular training differences," she announced, catching up to him once again. "For instance, fewer women maintain active strenuous physical activity after adolescence. Fortunately, that's beginning to change. On the other hand, Dr. Kenneth Cooper maintains that hearts and lungs and blood vessels have no sex. That's reassuring now, don't you think?"

Walter was starting to slow. "Hooking up with another runner is a good idea, I believe," Effie told him. "It allows one to share the frustration, the aches and pains, as well as the joys of running."

Sweat poured off Walter's brow.

"My, it's warm," she announced.

For miles she jogged happily after him. The last mile of the race Walter took off. In a blaze of glory, Effie thought, leaving her in the dust. And then she became irritated with herself for thinking in clichés. And irritated as well that he assumed he could leave her in the dust.

She sent messages to her oxygen-depleted muscles to catch up. Working hard, she narrowed the gap between them. "Walter," she yelled. "Wait up!"

Walter bypassed the finish line and ran right through the park down to the ocean, where he dove into the Pacific.

Effie ran down the beach after him. "Walter," she yelled again. "Walter, wait up!"

She stood on the sand and watched him swim far out to sea. It looked as though he were heading for Catalina, but that of course, was impossible, being over twenty-six miles away, and Walter was already spent.

Effie was patient. When he swam down the beach, she trotted after him. When he swam back, she matched him.

Twenty-two minutes later Walter emerged from the water, blue and shivering and defeated. "You think you're an iron man, Walter? You think this is some sort of triathlon? I don't think you should have stayed in so long. Extended exposure is dangerous for a man your age. You could easily have developed hypothermia."

Walter collapsed, face first, into the sand.

Effie walked over to him and whispered in his ear. "Stay away from co-eds, Walter." Then she turned and headed for the parking lot.

Chapter Sixteen

"Oh, my gawd! I can't believe you did that!" Blythe laughed at Effie's description of the race and meeting in the market.

"But isn't that considered stalking?" Lucy asked. She looked worried.

"I prefer to think of it as coincidence," Effie responded. "You know I race periodically."

"Yes," Lucy agreed. "But you don't normally drive forty miles out of your way to go to the market, do you?"

"Only in cases of necessity. I saw this as necessity. Walter needs to know he can't continue to hurt women without facing repercussions. Plus, I'd never endanger him."

Ramona agreed. "I know you well enough to know you'd never purposely hurt anyone, Effie, though a half hour in the ocean seems a little scary."

"His choice," Effie said. "Not mine. I kept pleading with him to get out of the water."

"I wish I could have been in that market," Blythe confessed. I would have loved to have seen Walter's reaction."

"Mostly he just hissed a lot," Effie said.

"I just don't want you to get arrested or sued or something," Lucy said.

"Oh, she can't get arrested for grocery shopping, Lucy. Or for running a race." Blythe laughed again.

"I came in eighth in my age group. My personal best."

"You see?" Blythe said. "Next time you go to the market, gal, I want to go with you."

"Agreed," Effie said.

🙥 🙥 🙥

Francine and Effie sat in the college cafeteria, ignoring the clatter of dishes and trays. "Get all those papers graded?" Effie asked.

Francine nodded. "Now it's on to the next set."

"I know; it seems endless." Effie, looked around and lowered her voice. "I have something to share with you."

"What is it?"

"I thought I was going to be fired. Second time I've thought this." Effie sat down. Her first experience with Administration followed an evening outing she planned for her literature class. A poet friend had apprised her of a local reading, and Effie made arrangements for students who attended to earn extra-credit points. To her surprise, many students showed up. Not known to her, however, was the fact that all the readers were lesbians. She was sure the religious college would unceremoniously bounce her out on her fanny.

"Don't worry about it," The dean of the English Department said, laughing. "No doubt a good experience for our students. Our job is to broaden their horizons."

"So what is it now?" Francine asked.

"You know how we were given a list of novel possibilities for the literature class? Fran nodded, her mouth full of blueberry muffin. "Well, I picked *Women in Love*. So I thought, if I'm going to teach this novel, why not show them the film? Anyway, after watching the flick, a student came up to me and said that he thought it was the most disgusting film he had ever seen, referring to the naked wrestling match between the two men."

"You showed that? Brave of you, gal." Fran took another bite of muffin.

"Yeah, I showed it, then worried all weekend that I'd be out of a job. But this morning when I told the dean what happened, he just laughed and said, 'Don't worry about it. Half of our students spend their evening watching the Playboy Channel.'" Effie paused. "Maybe I'm not meant to be an instructor."

"You're a terrific teacher, Effie. And I should know. I've been around long enough. Look at all the students who stop by the office to chat with you. Students don't do that unless they're afraid they're going to fail, or because they like you. Relax."

"Guess next time I should pick *Anne of Green Gables* or something."

Fran snickered. "Right. Except I doubt it's on the list."

ॐ ॐ ॐ

"What are you doing?" Effie watched Ramona, who sat at her kitchen table chewing on a pencil.

"I'm writing an ad."

"For?"

"A man."

"A man. A handyman? You don't mean man as in lover man, do you? Haven't you been listening to me these past few months? Too much trouble, Ramona. Too much pain and heartache."

"Hmmn. Agreed. But I feel that I'm willing to risk again."

"Brave woman."

"Or foolish one. Anyway, how does this sound? *Large and lovely SWF seeks passionate prince to dance the night away.* I thought I'd better mention my size upfront."

"Your size is fine."

"I'm not unhappy with it, but I figured I'd eliminate the ones who are looking for the anemic-sprite type." She looked at Effie. "Nothing personal. Do you like *large and lovely*? Sounds better than *pleasantly plump*, don't you think? Or *dowdy and dumpy*."

Effie laughed at her. "You are not dowdy or dumpy. How about *beautiful and buxom*?"

"Not bad. I think I'll use that." Ramona scratched something out on the paper in front of her. "Want me to write one for you?"

"And say what?"

Ramona thought about it a moment. "We could try, 'Suicidal sexpot seeks metaphorically- minded male.'"

Effie laughed.

Ramona went to the refrigerator and poured two glasses of orange juice. "I'm not *really* writing an ad. I was just reading them: speculating, thinking about what I'd want in a mate, should I want one again."

"And what would you seek?"

"Passion. A sense of humor. Kindness. Intelligence. Sensitivity."

"Sounds good, but recall Blythe's first husband. He was all those things *plus* being secretive and elitist. He thought the entire hospital nursing staff was his personal dating service, and yet everyone who met him thought he was the kindest man."

"I know. It's a dice toss, isn't it?"

"Yeah," Effie agreed. She looked at Ramona's list. "Don't forget *available*. After my experience that seems to be a primary prerequisite."

Ramona wrote down *available*.

Effie watched her, then added, "Order two to go."

ᔒᔒᔒ

Effie answered the knock on the door. Mandy stood there, tears trailing down her cheeks. "Mom, can I come in? Dad's being a jerk."

"Of course, kiddo, and tell me about it." Mandy collapsed on the sofa. Effie looked at her daughter. "Okay, how is he being a jerk?"

"He makes Megan and me do all the housework. We have enough work to do just dealing with college. And can you help me with a paper, please? I'm having a hard time with this dumb argument paper." She tossed some papers on the couch.

"I'm happy to take a look, Megan. But don't you think both you and Mandy can pitch in and help around the house?"

"Yes, but we're not his maids."

"I know that. I'm just making a suggestion. And yes, I can talk to your father, but I think it best that you and Mandy try first."

"Okay, but if he's still unreasonable, will you tell him he's being totally unfair?"

" I said I'll talk to him if necessary."

"Mom? Can I ask you something?"

"Of course, sweetie." Effie gently moved a curl out of Megan's face."

"Is there another…another man in your life? Is that why you left?"

Effie studied her daughter's earnest face. "I thought there was. Now I'm not so sure. But anyway, my leaving wasn't so much about him as about me. And please know that it was never about you and your sister."

Megan's eyes brimmed with tears.

"Your father is a good man," Effie continued.

"Do you still love Dad?" Megan asked.

"I'll always love him because he's the father of my three gorgeous children. I can't ever thank him enough for that. And I love him because of our earlier days when everything was new and we were busy raising you three. But we're apples and oranges; we want different things."

"I'm not sure I understand all this," Megan said.

"I'm not sure I understand either. I just hope that one day you can forgive me for turning your world upside down."

Megan nodded, all Effie felt she could hope for after what she had done.

"But know I'll always love you and your sister and brother. No matter what. Okay?" Effie reached over to hold her daughter. "Now let's take a look at your paper of yours. My guess is that I might have a suggestion or two. And when we're finished, let's make some dinner."

"Mom?"

"What, Sweetie?"

"Thanks for listening to me grump."

Effie hugged her daughter. "I thought that's what moms are for."

❧❧❧

She hid behind a headless statue in the university sculpture garden and waited. From her vantage point she watched him stroll the same campus pathway that not so very long before they had walked together, on Thursday evenings. She noted with some satisfaction that life without her was taking its toll. Walter looked deflated and tired. She let him pass, then ran after him, notepad in hand. "I'm only doing this because I want to write about it," she told him.

For an instant he stood there, confused. Then, in the glow of the overhead floodlight, she saw his face flush with recognition. He looked around for a means of escape. "I wore my sneakers, Walter. Anywhere you run, I can run too."

He resumed walking. "What are you doing here?"

"I have every right to be here. I, too, had a class this evening." She opened the small notebook. "Plus, as I said, I'm doing research. So tell me, exactly, what it is you are feeling at this moment in time."

He kept walking, staring straight ahead. "I want you to go away."

"Too bad. I have no plans of departing until I've completed this interview." She stopped in front of him, blocking the path. "I repeat, what is the emotional context of this surprise meeting?" She licked the tip of her pencil and looked up at him in eager anticipation of his answer. "Well?"

Effie was standing very close to him and she saw in his eyes that same crazed look wild animals get when you come upon them unannounced, the deer-in-the-headlights look. She was well aware that at any moment Walter might bolt. He put his hand to his forehead. "You must stop this, Effie. I'm no longer interested."

She ignored his plea. "Would you say you feel cornered? Would you describe the sensation as trapped or, perhaps, out of control?" She made notes on the paper.

He sighed. "Why are you doing this to me?"

"I told you. I'm going to write about it. I think of it as a guide to female students. Maybe I could have them printed up and handed out during registration." She stood on her tiptoes, attempting to look more evenly into his eyes. "It's too bad you never recognized that I was good for you in ways you don't understand." She sank back down again.

"I don't *want* to understand!" They had reached the parking lot and he pulled out his keys, opened the door to his car, and threw papers, books, and the lot inside. "Goodbye, Effie."

Before he could react, she scrambled up over the hood of the car and sat down on the top of his Volkswagen; she perched there like a praying mantis, a bug on a bug. "Get down from there!" he demanded.

"I will not."

A passing couple peered at the two of them curiously. The girl whispered something to the young man and they both laughed.

Walter could hardly contain himself. "Now look what you've done! People are laughing at us. I repeat, get down from there!"

"Can't make me."

"I can and I will. I'll call campus security and have you arrested." A vein in his right temple had begun to throb.

"Bully."

He lunged for her foot, but she was too quick for him. He lunged again and she caught him, slid her body off the hood and trickled down into his arms. It was hold her or let her fall. She laughed.

He jumped back as though attacked by a viper. "Damn it, Effie, go away!"

"Are you hungry? I'm famished. Let's go eat and finish the interview."

"I can't eat with you," he whined.

"Why not?"

"Because I can't, that's why not. Because I'm neither hungry nor interested. Because it's late and I'm tired and I want to go home." He sounded as though he might cry.

"To Ruth or to the dog and cat?"

"You have to stop this groveling," he told her. "It's most unattractive." His voice was firm, in command.

"Oh really? Nobody calls it groveling or unattractive when a man pursues a woman," she answered.

"It's anxiety-producing for a man to be pursued. I want you to stop." He noticed her thick curls bounce around her face.

Effie took out her notebook and wrote down his response. "I think I see what we're afraid of here. Five thousand years of acculturation comes into play. The hunter is threatened, is that it?"

Walter wrenched open the car door. "*We're* not afraid of anything, missy."

"Good, then I have a proposition for you."

Walter raised a skeptical eyebrow.

"Stay away from any more female students, Walter, or I go to administration and tell them about your unprofessional and unbecoming conduct. It's sexual harassment, that's what it is. I can tell them how I earned my A."

Walter blanched. "You were a willing participant," he snipped.

"As were all the others? Does any attractive woman in your class ever get a B?"

His look said it all. Effie laughed at him. "Your mother and I went to Hollywood Park last week. Did I tell you? She won the Exacta: seven hundred and twenty dollars. Not bad, huh? She sure was excited. I was too, of course, though not as much as she."

"Effie, there is too much pain in this for both of us. Please go away."

"All right, Walter; if that's what you want. But stay away from female students." Before he could blink, she walked off into the shadows of the parking lot.

❥❥❥

"I'm going to the Book Awards banquet Saturday night. My agent didn't want to go so she gave me her ticket."

"I'll be there as well," Julie said. "Do you want me to speak with you if I see you there?"

"Why wouldn't you speak with me?"

"Oh, some clients feel funny about conversations outside of therapy. And they don't want to have to explain who I am to others. I try to honor that."

"All my friends know I'm in therapy."

"Then if we meet, we can talk. And who knows? Perhaps someday they'll be acknowledging *our* writing efforts."

"Wouldn't that be great? Then I wouldn't have to teach anymore and you wouldn't have to listen to other people's problems."

"I like listening, if I feel I can help."

"Good. Because the question of the day is what sort of neurosis keeps a man in a relationship like he claims to be in with his ex-wife?"

"It's *your* issues that we're here to confront."

"I know, but right now he *is* my neurosis. I would like you to tell me what you think. I need to know so I can write about it with authenticity."

Julie chuckled. "Oh, he probably has some caretaking needs. Some guilt we don't understand. Perhaps she takes care of him. He's probably comfortable. No doubt they've worked out a system as many couples do. It sounds as though that's how he wants to live. And his staying has nothing to do with you."

"It has to have *something* to do with me."

"Why? Why can't you accept that the man has his own limitations, apart from feelings for you? From what you've told me, he hasn't left his cozy home for other women either, and most likely isn't going to."

"What you are saying is that there is nothing I can do about it."

"Exactly. There is nothing you can do to change things. You can only change yourself. No woman is going to make him leave. For whatever reason, he's obviously getting something there or he wouldn't stay. People have mysterious connections between them."

"Hell, most connections are neurotic; you said so yourself."

"I don't believe I used that word, but yes, I probably said something to that effect. Tell me about the tears I see."

Effie sniffled. "I can't cry today; I have a job interview after this with another school."

"I rarely see you cry."

"I've cried so much, I'm empty of all liquid."

"In here, I've only seen itty bitty tears."

"That's because after forty it takes all day to make the necessary facial repairs. Crying is hell on the appearance. Ramona has these herbal teabag thingies you put on your eyes, but I'm not convinced they help much."

"Effie," Julie said gently, "how would you like to be his wife, or ex-wife, or whatever she is?"

Effie hiccoughed. "I don't think he's interested."

"No, that's not what I meant. How would you like to be *her*? Imagine what that must feel like."

"It can't be any worse than this."

"It might be useful for you to use your empathy and imagination to see how her experience and yours might be the same. Or how they are different. Perhaps you could try writing something from what you imagine to be her point of view."

"I never thought of that. I'll give it a try. Thanks."

"And next week we can talk about what you've learned."

Effie frowned. "Some days I wonder if I'm learning anything."

Chapter Seventeen

Effie paced her small living room. Ramona watched her. "Settle down, Effie. You suspected all this stuff before."

"Suspecting is different from knowing for sure." She threw a pillow on the floor, then sat down and pounded it against the rug. "Oh, he is so disgusting! There's not an honorable bone in his body!" She tossed the pillow against the sliding glass door. "Why is it everywhere I go, *someone* knows Walter Rabinowitz and is happy to tell me all about him?"

"No doubt because you travel in the same circles."

"Is that some sort of metaphor for my life—traveling in circles?" Effie had just returned from an all-day writers' fair, where she had spent considerable time chatting with David Boyup, also a writer of fiction, as well as a part-time instructor at the university. Boyup was happy to have someone with whom to gossip, especially someone so intimately familiar with the writing program. Effie resisted telling him just how intimate.

They had run through the list of professors they knew in common, each commenting freely. "Do you know Connolly?" Boyup asked.

Effie talked to him writer to writer. "I've heard Connolly's a twit," she answered. "And offensive to boot."

"That was my feeling as well. Ever take a class with Walter Rabinowitz?"

Effie's insides jumped. "Yes," she answered cautiously.

"I've known Walter for ages," Boyup told her. "He's an ex-drunk, like me. I've been dry for sixteen years."

Effie felt her stomach catch. "Rabinowitz is an alcoholic?"

"Yep. He sure had the hots for Helen du Luc. You know her?"

Effie choked out an answer. "I don't think so."

"Grad student. Femme fatale. When Rabinowitz first saw her he stood there, shaking all over. 'I'm a divorced man,' he told me. And shook some more."

"I'm not sure Rabinowitz is divorced," Effie answered.

"Really? He told me he was."

"Maybe he is, then. But he still lives with his wife."

"Hmmn. Well, you know writers."

"I think perhaps I do know Helen du Luc. She's the TA for Bradford, right?"

"Maybe." And Boyup was off discussing some other person of interest to him. Effie nodded and attempted to listen, but her mind was busy putting together bits and pieces of information.

ॐॐॐ

"Why didn't he tell me he was an alcoholic, Ramona? I even asked him about it a couple of times because he seemed so familiar with the workings of AA, and because he never took so much as a sip of wine when we were together."

"Look, from what you've told me, he's not the sort of guy who admits any weakness. Why be so surprised?"

"Because it hurts that he'd keep such vital information to himself, that's why. Because that's a pretty major thing to know about someone. Because he didn't feel free to tell me. Because he assigned addictions to me. 'Are you sure you don't have some sort of eating disorder?' he asked. Because I was always too nervous to eat in front of him. Because I'm skinny. The only addiction I've ever had is *him*. At least I'm honest about it. Is the word gullible written on my forehead?"

"If you want to know what I think, I think you're addicted to the hope of finding the perfect love. Obsessed with it. Most women discover what you're discovering at eighteen or twenty, or when they divorce at twenty-eight and the reality strikes."

"I feel as though I've been ensconced in a convent for the last twenty-six years."

"I guess marriage can seem like that."

"Terrific. I feel exceedingly foolish learning all this at my age."

"Better your age than ten years from now."

"I wonder," Effie said, playing with the fringe on the pillow she had retrieved, "I wonder if I was better off believing the world was cotton candy. The other day I was out jogging and I met a neighbor, seemed like a nice guy. The first twenty-five words out of his mouth were that he lived down the way with his wife, but they were getting a divorce. Sure they were. It's no wonder I'm always involved in adversarial relationships with men; they all seem to be lechers."

"Some are, Effie, but not all. I refuse to believe that."

"David Boyup is a nice man. He's the teacher who told me about Rabinowitz. I hate having to suspect all men."

"Right now, dear heart, if I were you, I wouldn't trust myself to cross the street alone. You are an infant in these matters. Your judgment is lousy."

"Thank you very much."

"What are friends for but to tell you the truth? So, do you know this Helen person?"

"Helen du Luc. Isn't that a pretentious-sounding name?"

Ramona giggled. "Sounds like a stripper's nom de plume."

Effie sat cross-legged on the floor. "I could never figure out whether or not she was beautiful. She is thin with a ballerina's body."

"At least he runs true to type."

"I've never been called a femme fatale in my life!"

"My reference was solely to body type."

"Oh. Helen du Luc has an extremely high forehead. I suppose he read into that some superior intelligence."

"What is she like?"

"I barely know her. I think she was the dean's spy. Once we got into a disagreement over the inane enrollment procedures. She has a peaches-and-cream complexion. By the look of her, she never ventures outdoors."

"Hmmn. Healthier that way. Were her eyes pink?"

"You mean like bunnies? God, Ramona, what if they screwed like bunnies? Goddamn him!"

"Effie, even though, from what you've told me, I can't stand the man. Still, in all fairness to Walter, just because he was attracted to her doesn't mean he screwed her."

"Big deal. He wanted to. Goddamn him!"

"The bastard."

"Don't say bastard. Or son of a bitch. It's a denigration of the female."

"All right then. The prick."

"That's better. That holier-than-thou prick. I even asked him, 'How do I know you don't pick out one student every semester?' 'You know better than that,' he said."

Ramona peered at her. "Right. He picks one out every third or fourth semester because it takes that long for the process to work. In your case it sounds as though he picked *two* out at the same time."

"To hell with him! And Helen du Luc. She always wears bright red lipstick. Damn him to hell." Effie threw the pillow once again. "I've decided she wasn't beautiful, just young."

"With provocative red lips."

"Yes. Why is it that men like him can have any pretty young number they want hanging on their arms?"

"Because there are thousands of women trying to fall in love with Daddy all over again."

"Wonderful. I feel taken in, Ramona. I *believed* him, every lousy gorgeous word. It was all lies. All he wanted was to screw without complication."

"So now you know. So now you can let go of your illusions."

"I've been trying to. Damn it! He made sure I bought into those illusions hook, line, and sinker. Oh, he is abominable!"

"And you were very vulnerable."

"Yes, a vulnerable, but willing participant. Too willing. Perhaps that was my attraction. It's no fun stomping all over a crusty cynic. Maybe in his late fifties he can no longer attract a twenty-year-old, but he can attract a woman in her forties, who is only slightly used, having married young. I think I'm pretty well preserved for a mother of three."

"I agree."

"That's another thing he told me. 'I enjoy the company of *mature* women,' he said. 'There's sort of a musty aroma that surrounds them.' And he smiled seductively."

"I think I'm going to be ill." Ramona made a face.

"I wish I had been, all over his corduroy jacket with the patches on the elbows. Instead I fell for that line. 'That's just decay,' I joked. Women of the world, forgive me. I knew not what I did. He knew just what to say, what buttons to push."

"Of course he did, Effie. Look at the years of practice he's had." Ramona picked up the tossed pillow. "Why do you suppose his wife, ex-wife, whatever, puts up with him?"

"I can't figure that part out. Because she's quickly approaching the prehistoric years as far as men are concerned. Maybe he takes care of her, or vice versa. Most likely vice versa. My therapist says she probably has nurturing needs. Maybe she loves him. Maybe the two of them are so wrapped up in their Eastern-religion stuff that she doesn't notice. Maybe she's transported herself to other dimensions." Effie paused. "Edward Hines told me there's no sex."

"Why would Walter tell him that?" Ramona looked perplexed.

Effie thought a moment. "Perhaps to excuse his philandering?"

"Makes sense. Wonder if it's true?"

Effie threw the last pillow from the couch against the wall. "They believe in reincarnation, which leaves me with one minor consolation prize."

"Which is?"

Effie spoke, enunciating every word. "Well, if there is such a thing as poetic justice, and I'm praying to the mother of the universe that there is, then I am firmly convinced that next time round Walter Rabinowitz will return as a slug—a slimy, low-down, good-for-nothing banana slug."

"Hey, slugs need love too," Ramona chuckled. "I'll bring the salt."

"Salt?"

"When you were a kid, didn't you ever pour salt on snails and slugs?"

"No, I did not. I think that's disgusting." Effie shuddered. "I move banana slugs off the trails so hikers and bicyclists don't run over them."

"Well, as a kid, my mother paid me a penny apiece to rid her garden of snails. I'd sprinkle salt on them and then sit back and watch them foam and sizzle.," Ramona said.

"I'd be happy to think about Walter sizzling."

"I thought you weren't coming from a place of bitterness and revenge," Ramona said.

"I've changed my mind. Ramona, damn it, how does one compete with sainthood?"

Ramona looked at her dear friend sympathetically. "Probably by remaining an impossible dream."

Chapter Eighteen

So you were taken in by pretty words. Somewhere you read that writers are open, helpless creatures with no real understanding of what they have written and therefore believe everything that is said about them. To this you add, *to* them. It's easy enough to assign blame, to avoid taking a look at the consequences of one's own actions. The truth is, you were so easily persuaded.

You try not to lie. Does fiction count?

৬৬৬৬

When the recognition that another man was important in her life first surfaced, Effie struggled with the pain and ultimately told her husband everything, thereby causing him pain. She could not divide herself that way, even though Ramona had suggested that an affair might have brought to light the truth of Walter, and at the same time, saved her family much grief.

Is it possible to love two people at a time, or is it difficult enough to love, to really love, just one? Effie asked herself this question repeatedly. For a romantic, raised in the era of Rock Hudson and Doris Day walking hand in hand off into the sunset, the set-up for her was complete. Do couples really share such love for a lifetime? When Walter had first expressed his interest to Effie, she wrote to him:

I keep thinking about you. How we have complicated things! Some tentative conclusions, which I know could fly out the window the next time we meet. I just read somewhere that the French say that without adultery, there is no novel. What a rationale for two writers! Despite that, I recognize that to come to you from a place of subterfuge and dishonesty would only serve to negatively color a relationship I choose not to jeopardize, a relationship I have come to cherish.

This is so hard: wanting you, in some sense needing you, and yet recognizing, not out of any moral context or convention but rather out of something much more elusive, how much we stand to lose. God, the pain of this! Either way we forfeit! In the pit of my being I feel this, so I keep you to myself; you are my fine secret in a life that seeks not to hide. Back to square one: Do not collect two hundred dollars, do not pretend.

Mandy, as a three-year-old, had two imaginary friends. We had marvelous tea parties. Mandy's two pals always disappeared the moment her brother and sister returned from school.

I, too, long to disappear like a kite set free: to soar, unfettered. And I long not to hurt anyone, but how is that possible?

His response pounded in her ears. He said to her, "I love you with conscience and responsibility."

But she could see now that he had loved her only when it had been convenient to do so. Unconditional love, another favorite term of Walter's, meant loving no matter what, did it not?

Still, she misses him, misses his letters, which Effie acknowledges were fascinating missives. Her skin hurts when she acknowledges to herself that the real meaning of intimacy is not being afraid to dig your heels in.

"How many chances do you think we get to throw love away?" She had asked him this once back when they were still close.

"I don't know," he said. Facing the fact that his unwillingness to dialogue meant he never really loved her, is for Effie, an ache beyond reason, an ache beyond time.

෨෨෨

Walter Rabinowitz was a dark place, an underworld from which she had to escape. Her despair, as well as her feelings of revenge for the betrayal, all stemmed from that dark spot in her soul. She knew that absence of light was but a momentary matter: this time of suffering was a period in which she would gain something of value, and that she would renew herself and grow.

If only it didn't take so long.

ॐ ॐ ॐ

"What if we run into him?"

"What if we do?" Effie grabbed Ramona's arm and propelled her toward the English office building. "I need these papers. I have every intention of finalizing a few things so I don't ever have to set foot on this campus again. And I'm not going to put my life on hold, quit going places just because of Walter. Most particularly not because of Walter."

"What if we see him?"

"Then I greet him with grace and tact and style. Then I clunk him on the head. Come on, I don't have all day."

Ramona waited around the outskirts of the English Department while Effie went about her business. Twenty minutes later Effie emerged from the building. "All right. Let's go. But first I have to go to the bathroom."

"You always have to go to the bathroom!"

"It's this health program I'm on: twelve glasses of water a day. What goes in..."

Effie led the way to the closest women's bathroom. "Some of this graffiti is pretty neat, Ramona. I bet someone could get an entire book out of the sayings on bathroom walls."

Ramona, washing her hands, looked around for her friend. "Effie?"

Effie did not answer.

"Effie?"

"Ssh. I'm busy."

"Busy?" Ramona asked, suspicious. "Busy doing what?"

"Creating a little graffiti of my own. Why didn't I think of this sooner? It's enormously gratifying."

Ramona banged on the stall door until Effie opened it and pointed to her art work.

"Well? What do you think?" Effie pointed to her handiwork, scrawled in red ink on the door.

Ramona read aloud. "'Walter Rabinowitz is an egomaniac, a creep, and a lousy lay.' You can't write that!"

"Why can't I?"

"You'll get arrested, that's why!"

"I'll get arrested for writing the truth?"

Ramona shook her head. "You have just defaced university property! I'm leaving." She grabbed Effie's arm.

"I'm not leaving yet." Effie proceeded to the next stall and wrote nasty things about Walter. "When I'm finished here, Ramona, we need to go over to Building B."

"I'm telling you to stop this."

"It's washable. No permanent harm done to the door. Imagine what we'd see in the men's room."

"Effie, stop this. You are being ridiculous. You are not fifteen."

"But I *feel* fifteen." Happiness rang in her voice. "And I feel justified, friend. I feel entirely justified. Other students need to know who he is, young ones in particular."

"You know what it's time to recognize? It's time to recognize that this guy really did not give two hoots about you. You've been settling for crumbs, and you deserve more. This fixation of yours is totally out of hand. It's time to start loving yourself. What about your kids? Your work? Your writing?" Ramona glared at her.

"I know you're right," Effie answered finally. "I just have to figure out *how*."

Satisfaction, she knew, did not come from scribbling on doors, from writing voluminous letters, from tearing after the man in races. Satisfaction continued to elude her.

She felt like yelling at him in public, hurting him as he had hurt her. Julie suggested a more positive approach, writing down her resentments in her journal. Effie tried that. The list went on until her hand ached, until she finally realized that it was not just Walter she was raging against.

There was little point to her overreactions. Instead of feeling better, she felt worse, felt embarrassed and uncontained and on the edge. And yet, her feelings were legitimate: She had every right to feel hurt and angry and betrayed.

ॐ ॐ ॐ

Then there was James, who, in Effie's opinion, was going quite mad. "After I split," Effie told Ramona, "for his birthday he bought himself a sports car."

"Which birthday?"

"Forty-eight."

Ramona nodded. "It figures. What color is the car? Red?"

"Gold. Another golden phallus."

"God."

"For my birthday he bought me a filing cabinet. Do you think there's something wrong here?"

"Well, you haven't exactly been a model wife."

"That's true, but it's more than that. When I think back on it, I've never owned a car of my own. I always got the one James thrashed. And as long as a car gets me from point A to point B safely, I don't much care about the rest. But now I realize that a car is a symbol of how I was never consulted, how James just went ahead and did or bought whatever he wanted."

Though Effie understood the variations of male midlife crisis, still she remained notably cynical about the process. "I wish somehow I could remove myself, stand back from the situation with James. From a distance, all of this might seem more amusing."

"I doubt it."

"He's working out as well. He's lifting weights, moaning and groaning about the pain of it. Then he struts around showing off his chest. I swear, Ramona, if he starts wearing chains around his neck and his shirt open to the navel, I'm going to puke."

"What is it about his behavior that bugs you so much?"

"I guess I expected more from him. He's buying new clothes too. Lots of them. Hand-monogrammed shirts. Is that so he knows who he is? Is he afraid some guy will walk away with his shirt at the gym?"

"Do you think it's possible to emerge from this unscathed, Ramona? I can no longer relate to the man. James has even taken to eating in those quaint cafés on Melrose, the ones that charge a fortune for a tuna sandwich. He's become a vain male in crisis."

"Seems to me you're attracted to vain men."

"It seems. Suppose this is some sort of test and I'm failing?"

Effie had spent a great deal of time pondering the heroine's journey, wondering if the choices we make really matter. The quest was one in which she, as sojourner, sought insight and power. James had not understood, had equated a woman's power as power *over*, instead of power *to*. She understood the concern of men who for years had abused power. Every enemy faced is in reality a negative part of one's own nature, something that seeks to defeat us. Walter built walls hoping to protect himself from the onslaught of Effie, who was quick to point out that walls are built most often to exclude the enemies of one's own temperament. The greatest hurts are those which cut through us and allow us to see ourselves.

Effie believed that on the path the seeker hopes to find or to rediscover what is meaningful. But how hard it was to hold on to values in trying times. What did she value? For one, the belief that love bears all things, endures all things. The belief that love is eternal, though we are not. Had she been acting those values as of late? She thought not.

Above all else, she sought unity. The goal was to meet the challenges presented and to maintain a sense of harmony and wholeness. Why was it that it seemed men were the ones who threw obstacles in her way? Was it true that we cycle through situations that bring us back to what needs to be met and overcome?

When Effie was a very small girl, no more than five or six, she learned a lesson, which, as lessons go, was an important one, one through time she thought she had forgotten. Her recent conscious treks through territory long since abandoned left her with memories as real as when the action occurred.

One evening when she was about six, a close family friend showed up at Effie's house with a boy whose family was visiting from Florida. Effie recalled Florida because she didn't know where that was and it sounded exotic and wonderful and she wanted that despicable eight-year-old to go back there immediately and return her father and "Uncle" Danny to her. Her father used to lift her up and let her hang from the beams in the living room. Her uncle used to do cartwheels all over the house to entertain her. Her wish had been that the horrible child from Florida would simply disappear forever, a wish that did not materialize. Instead the two men, along with the child's father, decided to treat the intruder to a night at the wrestling matches at Olympic Auditorium. Effie wanted to go. She had watched Gorgeous George on television; she knew all about wrestling, more than some stupid kid from a place she'd never heard of. Effie could even perform a hammer lock.

She pleaded. She cried. She sat in the car. "It's not a place for little girls," her father had told her. And he carried her bawling like a deserted calf back to the house and to the safety of her grandmother, who could not understand her desire, who knew nothing of the scissor hold.

"Come on. We'll make bread." Baking had been her grandmother's answer to every pain, real or imagined. The two of them set about kneading the dough. (Now, years later, Effie understood the therapeutic effect.) While she pounded and threw that lumpy mass around, her child's imagination envisioned every contact with the mat, every shove into the ropes.

Miraculously, her grandmother produced a tiny pan for Effie's very own loaf—the consolation prize. And by the time the dough had risen and they pulled it brown and sweet-smelling from the oven, Effie was no longer fuming. Certainly only a very special girl could produce such magic! They left their creations on the counter to cool.

The next morning she ran to the kitchen, eager to show off, to show *him* her effort.

"Where's my bread?" she asked her grandmother, who stood at the sink washing dishes. Her grandmother's two loaves sat on the counter where she had left them. "Where is it?" she asked again. Her grandmother pointed to the small pan soaking in the soapy water. "Where is it?"

"Your father ate it."

Effie stared at her in disbelief. "He ate *my* bread? There were two big loaves. Why would he eat mine?"

And her grandmother, the great mollifier, tried to explain that he had been hungry when he came in and that Effie's bread smelled good and was just the correct size for a midnight treat. "He thought you made it for him," she said.

Effie recalled thinking that her father had not even asked her.

So Effie learned at a very early age that there were things boys can do that girls are not supposed to attempt. And she learned that unless one is very careful, men will without hesitation, devour your efforts, gobble them up and thank you later for your kindness in creating just for them.

As she thought back over the jigsaw puzzle that was her life, as she pieced together the collage of incidents, she realized that her created version of the past was tangible. And Julie helped her to see the patterns as they emerged.

Another event thirty years before, played out at the Jonathan Club, an all-men's association in the heart of Los Angeles, resonated on the same level as the bread-baking incident. Effie's father had taken her there for dinner. The journey from the ground floor of the club to the restaurant, was made by elevator, one for men and one for women. Another ride in the back of the bus. *Little girls do not go to the Olympic Auditorium or ride in the men's elevator at the Jonathan Club.* Effie had argued. She made a fuss. Her father attempted to make it special, an elevator of her very own. But she knew; even then, she knew.

"Are you trying to say that even then you had a developed feminist consciousness?" Julie had asked.

For Effie it hadn't been an issue of feminism but rather one of separation. "I'll meet you at the top," her father had reassured her. And a calm, fur-bedecked woman took Effie under her mink wing and together they traveled to the top. "See?" Her father grinned at her as the door opened. "I told you I'd be here." After dinner they walked down the many flights of stairs to the parking lot because her father had had no idea how to counter the emotionalism of a big-eyed, notional kid.

She had never been gracious about separations or about slights, real or imagined. She had never been gracious about anything. And if Walter had only been willing to talk to her he might have known that fact, might have found some other more compassionate way to end the relationship.

Effie had quit humming "Some Day My Prince Will Come." She was learning about losing. Go back two spaces for believing he was leaving his wife. Spend painful hours figuring a way out of the penalty box.

Chapter Nineteen

Effie sat down to write. The terror and the solitude that is the writer's life is also the suspicion that one is out of step with everything and everyone: out of sync. Could she move the reality, or, at the very least, make use of it? Would anyone care? What did hundreds of pages, the hundreds of hours invested amount to? The desire to come closer to oneself resulted in alienation and separation from others. That was her reality. "To the work you are entitled, but not the fruits thereof," said Krishna to Arjuna in the *Bhagavad Gita*. Was it some sort of romantic trust in what she had to say that caused her to persist, when often even the intrinsic reward seemed nebulous and out of reach?

Perhaps that's what being in love gave her, the promise of rescue from herself. She knew she was not so different from thousands of other women who sought true passion, because a woman ought to have true passion; all the books said so! And Walter had been the perfect literary model because his own romanticism predisposed him to her romantic interpretations.

To hell with it, she thought. Perhaps the search was nothing more than soothing a bruised ego. Or perhaps the problem rested with the myth itself, not with her continued failed attempts to make love perfect. The princess held so many expectations.

"Women," she wrote, "are acculturated to invest more of themselves in relationships than men." Then she scratched it out. Big deal. Belaboring the obvious got her nowhere. Assigning the white knight as prototype for Walter was most certainly a dangerous practice, for she had made him what he was not. No wonder he had balked. And it had never before occurred to her to credit the reality of his pain, which is what self-absorption gave her: literary comparisons only she could live with. Surely the man had pain, didn't he, or had she fallen for an emotional dummy? And if so, why had he been so damn attractive to her? Did that mean that she, too, was emotionally lacking? As she had come to see, she was an expert in doing the emotional work for everyone else, so no wonder Walter had appealed, a man who seldom visited the realm of emotionality.

Perhaps the systematic difficulties she faced in loving him had to do with unfulfilled longings that would always remain unfulfilled, regardless of who wore the armor. Not a pleasant thought. To be a woman, or at least a wife and mother, often meant self-denial. To be a writer or a serious artist required assertion. Ah, the quandary. Maybe Edward Hines' comment to her regarding squelching the woman was his recognition of the problem, or was she giving him too much credit? Be the warrior, not the wounded; be the poet, not the wife. And if a woman wanted it all?

Effie decided to write a short story about a woman she did not know personally, although she knew of her pain. This individual, an instructor at the university where Effie worked, had, if hearsay could be trusted, left a tenured position at a small prestigious college, left an attentive husband and two children to follow a writer halfway across the United States. How she was received upon arrival was not exactly clear, although rumor had it that while the man had not been prepared for her precipitous and unexpected appearance, neither had the woman been prepared for the fact the writer had a wife. Oh, that nasty sin of omission.

There were enough parallels between the teacher's sad tale and Effie's own to intrigue her. The fact that the man in question died an early death did little to assuage Effie's belief that there was not much justice in this life.

From every word she wrote, she learned. Was it possible to write a story composed solely of existential moments in which there was no ending but rather an evolution toward new meaning? A story that had no conclusion, only reflection, was not likely to satisfy the majority of readers. *They were suspended in time*, instead of *and they lived happily ever after*, simply would not fly.

She found it all terribly depressing, almost enough to make her lay down her pen and take up work as a florist, work she thought she might enjoy for the pure sensual experience of spending all her time with flowers.

So where was the heroine on her journey? Certainly Effie had traveled through separation and alienation, which left her currently in a never-never land. Where was the creative insight, her undying faith that an answer did exist? Where was the transcendent function Carl Jung wrote about, the *thing* that arose from the subconscious to solve her difficulty?

Effie had seen Walter as that rescuer, had imbued him with transcendent powers. What a joke that was. How did one go about maintaining a sense of self? As a child she had been sustained by the belief, the inner myth that things would get better.

What was she doing now? Incubating. Thinking about the true cost of things. What something cost, she decided, was measurable by what was forsaken in order to have it. Walter had once commented, "Guilt sucks," and then proceeded to engage in a lengthy diatribe re: the Judeo-Christian tradition, which she listened to with some fascination, but did not for one minute, accept. Of course Walter would say that; it made his actions intellectually manageable.

Her tendency to sit back in quiet acknowledgment of the male point of view, even when she disagreed with the speaker, was, she was beginning to recognize, a serious difficulty. It wasn't that she didn't dare disagree, though she rarely disagreed in person. Effie liked to mull over issues, collect her thoughts on paper and organize her response. Walter would leave the comfort of her warm nest no doubt secure in the belief that they were communicating beautifully, and two days later be hit by a missive that said in effect, "In my opinion, your opinion stinks." Zingers, James had called them. Walter reacted by withdrawing.

Was it an act of dishonesty on her part to delay reaction? She knew this behavior stemmed from her volatile adolescent relationship with her father, who allowed her little feedback without threat of punishment, so she took her grievances to her journal, where, in no uncertain terms, she gave the man hell. The viper's tongue was not silenced, merely rerouted.

In ninth grade the major male authority figure in her life, aside from her father, was Mr. McKenna, her drama teacher. One afternoon, McKenna, exasperated by the enthusiastic hi jinks of his youthful cast members, threatened to cancel the play in which Effie had a starring role. "Any more fooling around and there will be no play!" McKenna had yelled at his cast of hopefuls. Effie burst into tears. The other students huddled in groups of three or four and quietly discussed the situation. "Effie," McKenna said finally, "go to the bathroom and wash your face." She obeyed dutifully, but she did not return to class.

One by one McKenna sent each female cast member into the restroom to root her out. Effie refused to budge. When he ran out of girls, the drama coach enlisted the help of a very embarrassed Jack Jones, class president, who walked into the girls' bathroom wielding an apology from the teacher and a plea that Effie please come out. "McKenna's not mad at you. Honest."

"No," she sniffled.

"Please."

"No."

"Well, I'm not staying in here, that's for sure." By that time Effie's tears had turned to wracking sobs and a frightened Jack hurried back to class to report that Effie was still crying.

McKenna himself barged into the bathroom and yanked Effie out of there, begging her to stop crying. "Effie, what's going on? I'm sorry." McKenna put his arm around her and pushed her out of the bathroom. "It's okay. Stop crying."

But she didn't stop crying. Exasperated, the teacher then escorted Effie to the office where the principal stuck smelling salts under her nose and told her to lie down in the nurse's office. In the next room she could hear the principal grilling the teacher as to his part in the drama. If the instructor, a bachelor, was bewildered, having never before encountered adolescent hysteria, so too was Effie.

The performance went on as planned, the only difference being that from then on McKenna treated his star as though she were constructed of some fragile diaphanous material, which when Effie thought back on it, was a predictable though incorrect assumption. What she learned from the entire experience was that while given to fits of uncontrollable tears, she was nonetheless tough as nails. In her English class, which McKenna also taught, she wrote a short story about a student who had a serious conflict with a teacher. McKenna gave her an A on the paper, commented on the verve and enthusiasm she brought to the telling, and continued to tiptoe around her. Thinking back on it later, Effie realized she must have had a serious crush on her instructor.

The tendency to overreact to men in positions of authority did not emerge again until many years later when she took a job as a teacher's aide in a special education class. One of her functions was to hand out candy every twenty minutes as part of a reward system. This task she found so onerous that she was soon called before the director to account for her actions.

"Tell me," the director asked, "what you think of my program." Effie recalled that he pronounced *my* as if he were B. F. Skinner himself.

"Philosophically," she answered him, "I'm opposed."

The director, a large man by any standards, glared at her over his desk. "Then what are you doing in my classroom?"

Effie felt herself weakening though she stood firm. "The best I can," she answered.

"Why are you philosophically opposed?"

"Because," Effie cleared her throat, "because children are not pigeons to be placed in a Skinner box and manipulated." Why hadn't she just kept her mouth shut, kept her opinions to herself? Why did she have to confront him, knowing ahead of time she was locked into a no-win situation? A smarter woman would have praised him to the hills, and then gone back into the classroom and done what she thought was right.

"I'll have no love relationships with students developing in my classrooms!" he had bellowed at her.

"That strikes me as the only sort of relationship worth having," Effie had responded.

She failed her interview. And because she could not stop crying, they sent her next door to the district psychologist, who listened with some interest, as well as amusement it seemed to Effie, and handed her a Kleenex. In response, she quit her job—they didn't dare fire her—and wrote a lengthy letter to the program director in which she reduced his book, *Reluctant Learners in the Classroom*, to an absurdity.

"Do you earn checks that allow you to choose one (modified) friend with whom you may eat lunch?" she wrote to him. "What happens if you display maladaptive behavior, that is, inattention, daydreaming, boredom, disruption? Do you spend minutes in isolation in a room adjoining your office?" (All of these behaviors were catalogued in his book; Effie simply borrowed them.)

Believing in a philosophy of living as a basis for action was not always easy. The director could keep his "program," which stressed neatness, discipline, conformity. To the director, the essence of education was his precious program, which struck Effie as backward.

Being a purist was a damn bumpy road to follow, but perhaps being a heroine meant making crucial painful choices, meant moving onward even when you didn't know where onward led.

Chapter Twenty

Effie followed Sunset Boulevard as it wound through Pacific Palisades to Brentwood. The tree-lined road meandered past elegant, substantial homes, one more beautiful than the next. An octogenarian Greek writer, whose works Effie knew only vaguely, was this year's host of the Books and Authors Awards.

She pulled up to a Spanish mansion painted salmon and turquoise. The house sat high on a hill. A broad expanse of emerald-green lawn rolled down to the street. A guard opened her door, asked to see her invitation, then whisked away in her car.

Effie followed the crowd to the backyard. People, wine glasses in hand, milled around an Olympic-sized swimming pool. White chairs had been set up around the pool and a speaker's lectern stood next to a fountain where three marble cherubs peed chlorinated water into the tiled depths. Effie smiled to herself, visualizing the losers soaking their heads in this Florentine decoration.

She surveyed the rapidly filling concentric rows of seats, hoping to see a familiar face. She felt a tap on her shoulder and turned around. There stood Nicholas, her writer friend, all smiles and cheese. He offered Effie a brie-covered cracker and said, "I thought wine and cheese gatherings were out." When Effie declined the goodie, Nicholas took another bite. "Pizza's the nouveau cuisine this year, isn't it?" Effie shrugged. "I'm going to get some more food," Nicholas told her. "Want something?" He motioned to the table holding an array of food-filled trays.

"No thanks."

Nicholas moved off. "See you later, then."

Effie found a waiter and accepted a glass of white wine. She had never been to a party amongst so many literary types before, many of whom she recognized. The primary intent of the gathered seemed to be to consume as much alcohol as possible while at the same time touting one's latest creative endeavor. She stood on the fringes of the party, a smile frozen on her face. She overheard a conversation in which an older woman said to the mustached man she stood next to, "Aren't you Dennis Mohr? I've read some of your books. Are you getting an award this afternoon?"

The man played with his moustache. "No," she heard him say as she trotted away. "I'm giving one. Best cookbook collaboration with a chef."

Wandering about, she heard snippets of conversation.

"So what is it, Frederick?" Effie listened as another woman spoke. "Do you want to publish my book or don't you?"

"I'm afraid I can't, Monica. I want you to know, however, that I remain a great admirer of your work."

"What do you know of literary creation, Frederick?" A man Effie presumed to be the writer's husband attempted to calm her. Monica brushed off his arm. "There's always some twittering publisher who thinks he understands artistic process."

"Monica," the man said, pleading.

"I'm just getting started, Howard," Monica responded.

Frederick started to move away. "Excuse me."

"I'm not finished, Frederick," the woman said. Effie moved quickly away.

"They seem to be starting," Effie heard a gentleman say to his companion. "Let's find a seat."

She looked for a chair. She spotted Julie in a back row. "Mind if I sit here?"

"Oh, Effie, hello." Julie looked a bit flustered. "Of course, sit down." On every seat was a handout explaining the awards. Effie took a cursory glance at the list, which seemed to her interminable. There were awards for every type of writing: autobiography, fiction, poetry, biography, best cookbook, children's book, etc.

A rotund man with a self-important expression on his face moved to the lectern and addressed the gathered throng.

Effie couldn't hear, but she decided that whatever he was saying was not worth moving up twelve rows. "We can't hear!" came the cry from someone several seats behind her. The man on stage fiddled with the microphone. A loud squeal from the audio equipment rang through the late afternoon air.

"Can you hear me now?"

"The man on stage, Gerard Cirlot," Julie whispered to her, "was at Stanford when I was. Different departments, of course. He was touted as the greatest thing since Faulkner. Published one novel. I don't think he's written anything since."

"That's Gerard Cirlot?" Effie studied the man. "I heard he reads around a lot."

Julie chuckled.

A loud round of applause greeted Cirlot as he handed an envelope to a young man who had loped up to the lectern. "What's his award?" Effie, who had been listening to Julie, had not heard.

"Poetry, I think."

"And to present the awards for biography..." The setting sun hit Effie right in the face, a poorly designed seating arrangement, she thought. There seemed to be no way to get away from its blinding presence. She put on her sunglasses. But the combination of wine, applause, and piercing light gave her a headache.

The process, as she feared, was indeed interminable. "They've got prizes for every sort of book known to man," Effie whispered to Julie. "Travel books, history books..."

"The awards for book reviewing are to be presented by..." Effie was half asleep, no longer listening to the voices droning on and on. "...Walter Rabinowitz."

Effie was instantly alert, frozen to her seat. Her heart pounded; sweat dribbled down between her breasts. She looked at Julie, who was beaming and clapping loudly. "Julie," she said in a voice barely audible. "That's him."

Julie leaned closer. "What, Effie? I can't hear you."

"I said that's *him*."

"Him who?" Julie asked, smiling as the man walked onstage.

"My ex-lover, that's who. Presenting the award."

Julie quit clapping and stared at Effie. "It can't be," she said.

"Why can't it be? It is. It's him, the professor."

Julie leaned over to Effie. "Effie, suddenly I'm not feeling well. I need to leave."

"Oh, Julie, feel better," Effie said, concerned. "Do you want me to help you to your car?"

"No, thanks. I can manage." Effie watched Julie hurry down the walkway.

"Feel better!" Effie yelled after her. She stayed and listened to the rest of the awards. As she was leaving the event, she felt a tap on her shoulder.

She turned around to see Walter glaring at her. "What are you doing here?"

"What am I doing here? My agent gave me his ticket, Walter. And for your information, I had no idea *you* would be here."

"I saw you sitting with Julie," he hissed.

"Yes. So? I believe I can sit with whomever I want. Anyway, why should you care where I sit?"

"It's not where you sit," he responded. "It's with whom you sit."

Effie was confused. "You know Julie?" At once Effie's brain went into overdrive, wondering if Julie was yet another one of Walter's conquests, though that seemed unlikely.

"Know her? I certainly do know her," Walter snapped. "I've known her all my life. Julie is my sister."

ϬϠϬϠϬϠ

"Looks as though I'm out one counselor, friend." The next morning, early, Effie was on the phone to Ramona.

"Why? What happened? I thought you were really making progress, Effie."

"I was. At least I was until yesterday afternoon when I went to an awards presentation and Julie was there and Walter was there and it turns out that Walter is Julie's brother."

"You're kidding!" Ramona started giggling.

"No, I'm not kidding and I don't think it's one bit funny, Ramona. I think Julie's now battling some personal crisis of her own. She's consulting *her* therapist. In the meantime, she called me said she can't see me anymore because of a conflict of interest. She's giving me a referral."

"Having a brother is a conflict of interest?"

"Having one you've called a schmuck is."

She said that?"

"Actually, I said it and she nodded. I took it as agreement from her. She made it perfectly clear to me that she thought my lover behaved in ways that hurt women. Which is true. And so now she has to deal with the fact that her brother is that very same jerk."

"Don't you think she suspected all this stuff about him before? Don't you think she knew about him?"

"I don't know. Maybe. She told me once that most people encounter problematic people in their lives, either family or friends. So what do I do now?"

"Carry on."

"I can't carry on, not like before, Ramona. My support system is missing."

"You are one of the strongest women I know. I'll be your support system when you need one." Ramona chuckled at the absurdity of it all. "Tell me again what Walter said."

"To hell with what he said. He was rude and angry and acted as though this was all my fault."

"Boy, I'd love to be the fly on the wall when he confronts her."

"I don't think Julie will say anything. Patient confidentiality and all that."

"This cements things though, doesn't it? More firmly than before. It gives Walter something else to blame me for. I've lost a lover, I've lost a therapist, I've lost a friend…"

"Wait a minute, Effie. Walter was never your friend, not really."

"That's the saddest part, Ramona. That's what I wanted him to be more than anything. More than a lover, I wanted the man to be my friend."

Chapter Twenty-One

Eucalyptus leaves hung heavy with mist, the result of the June dampness that pervaded early mornings near the coast. It would be noon before the sun broke through the fog and the day offered the promise of warmth. The charming, rustic old hotel nestled in the fog bank at the edge of the sea was the site of the annual Tri-Counties Writers' Conference. The phantasmagoric atmosphere enchanted visitors: The quaint inn was a perfect spot for indulging one's fantasies and illusions.

Winding narrow pathways meandered through manicured lawns, through well-tended flowerbeds down to the sea. Effie would not have been surprised to see Gatsby himself stroll the hedge-lined walkways, arm in arm with his Daisy, decked out in her summer finery, in her wide-brimmed straw hat.

Those most enraptured, caught up in the setting, were the conference leaders themselves, all of whom maintained a fraternity-like camaraderie, which was impossible to permeate. They fed each other's egos; in unison they became much greater than the sum of their parts. And, like fraternity brothers, the good ol' boys used the conference week to great advantage: The prettiest of the writing hopefuls were quickly singled out and invited to after-hour parties in hotel suites reserved for just such activities. *Wannabe* writers, seeking the path to fame and fortune, stopped first on their tour for a tour between the sheets, hoping to ensure their future success in print.

"I'm not feeling overly terrific about the two of us being here," Ramona announced to Effie as they strolled the hotel grounds. Initially Ramona had balked when Effie suggested they spend the day at the conference.

"I thought you were curious," Effie said.

"Not curious enough. With you at my side, I foresee a day of trouble."

"I need you to be with me, Ramona," Effie pleaded. And so Ramona had succumbed and let Effie drag her two and a half hours south of LA to the site of the Romanesque indulgences.

Now that the two of them stood outside the old hotel, Effie had a change of heart. "Let's walk down to the ocean." As they sat together on the beach beyond the hotel, Ramona played with dried seaweed, attempting to create a wreath of sorts.

"Maybe it was a mistake for me to come here," Effie said. She scooped up handfuls of sand and slowly released them, creating an ever-increasing mound next to her feet.

"I think perhaps you're right about that." Ramona twisted several strands of seaweed together.

"You do?"

"Yes. Are you asking to be hurt some more? Your Walter hurts people, Effie. He's a divorced Don Juan who acts as though he is married, or he's a married Don Juan who acts as though he's divorced. Either way, he's protected himself. So which way do you think it is?"

"I don't know. And I guess I should no longer waste my valuable time speculating. But I want to hear some of the speakers."

"I understand. But in either case, dear heart, I hope you get that he is unavailable and unattainable."

Effie could feel the hot tears starting behind her eyes. She threw a small stick to the tide and watched it disappear beneath the surge of the wave, and then bounce back to the surface. "Unattainable was part of his attraction, I suppose. The attempt to recreate past memory, the hope that this time I'd get it right. Only we never do."

Ramona put a generous arm around her friend and squeezed. "If it makes you feel any better, I don't think your guru is any closer to the divine soul than you."

"No?" Effie threw another stick.

"No. Because he creates new burdens for himself when he injures others."

"Maybe he doesn't mean to, Ramona. Maybe his actions are all in accord with his lifelong experiences. Isn't that what brings us to a certain point of understanding? I would like to believe that he is doing the very best he can." She shrugged her shoulders. "I once wrote that to him."

"That's fine, but his very best is not good enough for you." Ramona looked at her. "His best is not yours. And as long as he deceives himself, there can be no love."

"You think he never loved me?"

"Who can say? Most likely he loved the idea of you. Perhaps he loved you in his capacity to love you. Most certainly he didn't sound too interested in the challenge of love."

"A part of me will always be connected to him. But I'm angry too, because I wanted him to be my friend. I just hope that someday I can look back on this with kindness, that *he* can look back on this with kindness too." She stood up. "Let's walk a bit." Effie slipped off her shoes and held them in one hand. Ramona did the same. "With Walter I always felt as though I were taking a test. I did okay on the 'play-to-the-fantasy' exam, failed the 'crap-out-at-the-last-minute' quiz, okay on the 'state-of-bewilderment' test, and lousy on the 'logic' essay."

Ramona laughed. "Overall score, an F for my favorite friend."

Effie nodded and took Ramona's hand. "Maybe it was just all one grand paper-fuck."

Ramona turned to hug her and watched as Effie's tears flowed. "He wasn't capable of loving you, sweetie. You deserve more than what he had to offer."

Effie thought about this. She had sought access to Walter's most secret self, had wanted to combine spirit, passion, and intellect—had desired a journey to the centered life. But he had been terrified of that. Knowledge that love is primary, is the most-honored realm of the universe, did not interest him. His inner voice spoke a different language, one he had no desire to teach or to share with her.

The vision she had of Walter and his wife completed the classic picture: the two of them together, alone, in the house with the flowers and books, with the cozy fireplace, while she was on the outside banging on the bedroom door, wanting in. The discovery that he lived not in a quaint cottage with an English country garden and picket fence, but rather in a two-story stucco condo complex, both bewildered and saddened her. She spent so much time talking with her students about giving up their preconceived notions, and yet she had been unable to give up her own. She had been able to explain away his inability to leave his rose bushes, his carefully tended fruit trees, even though she herself had done so, but the reality of his lifestyle had been an awakening. There were no extensive flower gardens beckoning him. What kept him there was a connection Effie did not understand, one she had no access to. There she was again, banging on the bedroom door.

It had been so easy for her to make excuses for him, to give him the benefit of the doubt. When had he ever done as much for her?

"Do you think he hid behind financial concerns as an excuse for not leaving his ex?"

Ramona shrugged. "I think most of us are mired in the muck of our own making, economic or otherwise, because we choose to be. Not always, but often. The role of the struggling artist is very attractive to some, you know."

"But I don't think it's very attractive to men in their fifties. To them, money is power."

"From what you've told me about him, Walter felt powerful in other ways. And besides, what difference does it make?"

"I'm just trying to understand. I'm always trying to understand."

"Maybe some things are not meant to be understood. And the questions asked in an effort to clarify situations are construed as criticisms. It was a no-win for you, Effie."

She had come to see that what had attracted him was the conquest. And she had been so easy! Perhaps in time, she would no longer be obsessed by the grand spectacle of a love that had existed primarily in her head. Perhaps in time, the scent of sweet peas would not evoke memory. Perhaps she could put away forever the red high heels he had loved. Perhaps she could forget about mockingbirds and pomegranates and tree dahlias and eggplants and walks on the beach and the exquisite feel of his tongue on hers. Could she forget poetry and Mozart and classical guitar and Coleman Hawkins at midnight? Would the memory of sycamore leaves as broad as babies' faces, and the feel of his back against hers one day fade, dissolve into nothingness? That afternoon in the park had brought with it the recognition that she could no longer make grass sing as she had when she was a kid and played a tune for ladybugs. She blamed the grass.

And now, whom did she blame? Walter, for the bruise that sits on her soul? Herself?

It hurt to breathe.

"I guess I thought I could awaken in him a certain passion, but the dream wasn't real."

"Perhaps he was unable to truly share himself because he doesn't know what he's *able* to share, what his gifts are," Ramona said.

"Perhaps," Effie answered. "I tried to help him see that the things we are most afraid to share are our gifts."

Ramona smiled. "It seems to me that the writer is the artist whose work is most directly connected to feelings. But that doesn't mean he knows that. And that connection is what it takes to commit to work, to commit to someone you love. Here, blow your nose." Ramona handed her a tissue.

Effie looked at it. "Blue. Dyed again."

"You always have to be right, don't you?"

They looked at each other and both laughed.

"He was always talking about the importance of being open and vulnerable."

"Quit beating yourself over the head with this, kid. We know now that he talks a good game. And your lesson here is that you can't expect intimacy from another person, just because you desire it."

"The Buddha said 'Give up your expectations and you have all things.'"

"The Buddha wasn't in love. But he was right. People aren't always what we wish them to be, nor do they always act the way we'd like them to."

"Did I tell you   James took me to the Olympic Auditorium? He even made me a loaf of bread. We saw the wrestling matches that for almost forty years I've been replaying in memory. It was awful. We left after twenty minutes. But I love him for trying, for attempting to tie in to the past like that."

"Maybe that's all we can ask of another: the willingness to try."

Effie thought about Ramona's comment. With Walter she had allowed the hope to make love real. Her needs made him the romantic bard who swept her away to an enchanted world only the two of them inhabited: her vision of the white knight.

He had called her a witch because she talked to plants and animals, but the witch had been unable to engage him. She considered her witchery a fool's prize, fool that she was. Fool that she is.

And yet, when he came into the room, the light changed. Who could explain it? The process was no more rational than an act of creation.

Walter had offered her magical entry into the world of the imagination, had granted her unlimited visitation rights. And her letters to him had been journeys, explorations in which she pushed at the dimensions of consciousness, opened up to meanings beyond herself. Was that not love, or was the gift hers alone?

She had dared, had leaped blind into deep waters, journeying toward a comforting voice, relying on instinct. She knew the soothing stillness of the transparent liquid world, understood now, the awful clarity.

And so she pushed on toward the surface, mindful now, aware of the danger, on the lookout but always moving in the right direction: upward, toward the light, toward the shimmery effervescent glint of yet another transitory, enchanted moment.

§♥§♥§♥

Effie stopped and turned around. "We've come a long way, friend. Maybe it's time we head back." She looked down the long stretch of beach. "Let's go learn about the craft of fiction, listen to all those literary giants tell us their secrets."

Ramona gave Effie a cryptic look. "Haven't you experienced enough of that?"

Effie laughed. "Enough to know that ultimately it's all one grand fiction."

Chapter Twenty-Two

Huge Boston ferns draped the conference room of the classic San Diego hotel. Chintz-covered wicker settees beckoned the weary traveler to stop a moment and enjoy a brief respite, a peaceful interlude. Effie felt a sudden craving for a mint julep, which she imagined holding in one dainty, white-gloved hand.

Ramona looked around. "This place is unreal. It's like something out of an old movie."

"Exactly. All it needs is a fountain for Zelda to frolic in."

"Probably has one somewhere. When do I get a peek at Raskolnikov?"

Effie looked around the room and felt her pulse quicken. "Right now. Over there." She nodded in the direction of a group gathered around a sofa. Grabbing Ramona's arm, she pulled her behind a large potted plant.

Ramona giggled. "Now I'm starting to feel like Nancy Drew."

"The tall lanky one in the blue sweater," Effie whispered.

Ramona studied him through the leaves of the plant. "I can see the attraction. He has that rumpled, affected casualness artists seem to strive for. Beyond that, he's actually very ordinary looking." She took another peek at Walter.

"I didn't fall in love with his looks. Looks are secondary to me. They're not even secondary. They're tertiary, or what comes after tertiary? Anyway, I fell in love with pretty words as well as the belief that he meant them. I see now that he means them each time anew." She studied the names on the conference roster. "I wonder how many of these women Walter has known intimately?"

"Perhaps not that many if you consider his passion for vulnerable students. What fun is an equal? An equal is someone who is more likely to notice your disconnectedness and flirtatious nature. An equal is wise to the ways of dirty old men."

Effie sighed. "Are they all destined to become dirty old men? I hope not."

"Of course not. That's your fixation talking."

"The man has serial affairs, Ramona. They should put him on television. He probably Xeroxes his love letters to save time." The old pain resurfaced and she stood there in the grand room of the famous old hotel thinking it would not be too classy to be sick all over the flowered carpeting. Perhaps she *had* made a mistake in coming. Seeing him still hurt. "Oh, my god!"

"What?" Effie stared straight ahead. "What?" Ramona demanded again.

"The woman standing next to the lady in pink…in the green silk dress?"

"I see her."

"Helen du Luc, with the red lipstick," Effie said.

Ramona grabbed Effie's elbow and led her forward. "You are going to introduce me." The two walked toward Helen, who turned and gave Effie an appraising glance.

"Hello, Helen. Nice to see you here."

Helen raised one eyebrow, almost imperceptibly. "Effie, what are you doing here?"

"Me? Just some research. For a book."

"How fascinating." Helen looked dubious.

"This is my friend, Ramona. She's interested in the artistic process." The women eyed each other, sniffed out the terrain like two wary dogs on the beach, each waiting for the other to make the first false move.

"Actually," Helen continued. "Walter Rabinowitz invited me to the conference. You must know Walter from the program. He promised to introduce me to some agents and editors, friends of his."

"How nice of him," Effie said.

Ramona stepped on Effie's foot, a not-so-subtle warning for her to back off.

Helen went on. "I studied with Walter. We've become close friends. He's a charming man."

"Isn't he though? But one can't be too taken in by charm these days. It's simply not healthy, if you catch my drift."

Helen's already white face blanched whiter. "Healthy? Whatever do you mean?"

Effie leaned closer, whispering. "I'm only telling you this Helen, because we are both vulnerable women writers."

"You're only telling me what?"

"I have it on good authority that Walter has for the past several years, been having serial affairs with students."

"Serial affairs?" Helen looked worried.

"Yes. And I see it as my duty to women students to run an underground railroad of sorts, to get the women out of his way before he can strike. I know you're too smart to become involved with him, but perhaps you can pass the word around to save our compatriots from him."

"Thank you, Effie, for the information."

"Isn't it fascinating how it always seems to be the most charming men?" Effie turned and walked away.

Ramona giggled. "You are a mischief."

"Walter deserves it. And Helen du Luc will share. From now on, no female student will get within five miles of the man." Effie looked back toward the conference room crowd and was happy to see Helen sitting down, guzzling a large glass of wine.

"You know what bugs me about him the most? His propensity for summarizing the women he knows in one sentence. His many years as a book critic shows. *The school teacher's problem was that she was jealous and insecure.* Effie had sympathy for the teacher and could see how such insecurities were bound to surface in the company of a man such as Walter.

And now, she wondered, how was he summarizing her? She knew. She could hear him explaining away their relationship casually, to the next one in line, the next hopeful.

The problem with Effie was that she always had to be right, always had to have the last word.

Now she wished she had confronted him, asked him why he was continually concocting a problem for the women in his life. She knew why: so he never had to address his own culpability.

Effie looked up to see the director of the conference smiling at her, a professional jowly grin designed to welcome all visiting hopefuls. Effie smiled back and walked over to him. "You're Bennington Smythe." His smile broadened as he extended a huge paw.

"Yes. And you?"

She ignored the question. "You see that man over there, Mr. Smythe, the tall one in the blue sweater?" She took his elbow and twirled Smythe due west so he too had Walter in his direct line of vision.

"You mean Walter Rabinowitz?"

"Yes, I know who he is." Effie leaned into Bennington confidentially. "I don't think he's a very good man for your conference, Mr. Smythe."

"No? And why is that? Rabinowitz is a fine writer, a fine critic, a good teacher."

"Yes," Effie agreed. "He certainly is all of those things. But he's a philanderer. He screws around with his female students."

Smythe burst out laughing. "Which is precisely why I hired him, my dear. This conference would be nothing without a rake or two in our midst."

"Yes, well, word has it that he's not very good at it." Effie flounced away leaving Smythe still laughing. "He's as disgusting as Walter," she reported back to Ramona. "If such a thing is possible."

Ramona studied Smythe. "I think you're right. He just winked at me."

"Well, at least he knows some of us are on to the old boys' games. You know what my fantasy is, Ramona? My fantasy is that I gather together all of Walter's old loves. I'm sure we'd fill the hall."

"And what does he have to do, run the gauntlet while you and the crew pelt him with rejection slips and old love letters?"

"Nope. Worse than that."

"What? You roll him in contraceptive jelly? Soak him in a hot tub until he turns pruney? What?"

"Worse than that. He has to make all our fantasies come true. He has to stand by all the illusions he helped create. He has to love all of us the way he told us he loved us: unconditionally. He has to quit fooling himself. He has to expose himself and be open and vulnerable the way I was. He has to be willing to share more than just selective bits and pieces of himself. He has to be honest, and daring. He has to quit being afraid to love. He has to stop assigning blame to women for his continued failed relationships. He has to quit believing that the next time the next pretty lady will get it right, will be the adoring doormat he so fancies. He has to be there the way he said he'd be."

Ramona exhaled. "Boy, Effie. When's the guy supposed to write?"

❧ ❧ ❧

Bennington Smythe came to the lectern for the express purpose of introducing the next panel of speakers, whose topic was the business of writing. Top-name authors sat before them. Bennington tapped the microphone and the remaining crowd chose seats. How Walter had finagled a seat next to big name authors was not exactly clear, but on the other hand, not exactly surprising.

"Who does he think he is?" Ramona asked.

"Ernest Hemingway," Effie whispered back.

"Shh." A woman behind them tapped Effie on the shoulder and smiled a warning. Effie turned around and made a face at Ramona while Bennington Smythe introduced each panelist in turn.

After forty minutes of bantering and discussion of the literary life, the panel fielded questions from the audience. Walter twice brought Effie to hackles' rise with his flirtatious and funny responses to queries from an attractive woman seated in the first row.

A sweet-looking blue-haired woman in the back stood up and asked the panel, "How long should my manuscript be?"

Effie watched Walter, who was writing and not paying much attention to the audience. "What's he doing?" Ramona whispered.

"Most likely a crossword puzzle."

"*Now?*"

Effie recalled all the times Walter had called and asked for her help with a crossword puzzle. "What's Bambi's aunt's name?" And if Effie didn't know, she'd scurry about to learn that Bambi's aunt was named Ena.

"What do you say, Mr. Rabinowitz?" The woman in the front row addressed him.

Walter looked up, caught unaware. "Yes," he said assertively. "The answer is an unequivocal yes." He went back to his crossword puzzle. Several members of the audience snickered.

Effie recalled how intensely Walter disliked certain elements of the teaching process. Reading dreadful student stories, for example. Fielding questions he had heard a thousand times.

"How do you write a query letter?" someone else asked. Walter continued writing. He did have a natural ability for alienating those he considered dull and boring.

Effie stood up and addressed the famous writer-attorney on the panel, who in the past had won several palimony cases for famous actresses, and was now writing a book about his experiences. "If I wanted to use letters in a book, could you tell me, please," she asked, "who owns the copyright to letters? Is it the sender or the recipient?"

At the sound of her voice Walter looked up and straight at her. His face flushed red. She smiled at him and he quickly looked away.

"I'm not sure of the answer to that one," the attorney said. "Best you check with an attorney whose field of expertise is book contracts."

"Thank you." Effie sat down and watched as Walter's ears grew red. She grinned at him; he scowled at her.

"That was a pretty squirrelly answer," Ramona whispered.

"Guess he didn't know," Effie said. She sat in the conference hall, surrounded by writer hopefuls, consumed by a sadness, a rage at the overwhelming futility of her situation: her love for a person who no longer loved her back. The reality weighed heavily upon her. She no longer listened to the repartee, to the panel basking in the adoration of an attentive audience. Grateful applause roused her and she stood with the rest of the crowd, milling about now.

"I think coming here was a very bad idea," Ramona said. "Let's go home, or do you want to get something to eat first?"

Effie did not respond. Ramona reached for her arm to guide her from the hall, but Effie shook her off and walked to the front of the room, toward Walter who sat sparring with the same pretty woman from the front row.

"Effie," Ramona called softly. She hurried to Effie's side. "Come on," she whispered, "let's go home."

Effie ignored her and continued walking, dazed, hurt, functioning on empty. It no longer made any difference that she still found Walter fascinating because she now realized that he was all illusion who wanted no part of her.

"Effie," Ramona pleaded.

Effie continued walking toward the table where Walter and the other panel members were holding court. The bright light of recognition shone like a halo around her. Walter, surrounded by an adoring crowd, was in his element.

He looked up. Surprise and worry showed on his face. Not thinking, not really knowing what she was doing, Effie picked up the glass water pitcher that sat in front of the writer-attorney and upended the contents over Walter's brillant cranium. "Walter," she said, "you didn't want to be loved. You wanted to be worshipped."

The room was quiet. Those who witnessed the event watched Effie in stunned silence. Ramona hurried through the crowd and took her friend's arm. Effie no longer fought back the tears or the months of pretense. Ramona led her to the nearest exit.

Effie turned around for one last look at Walter, who sat there mopping the wet with a handkerchief, making jokes. "I guess she didn't like my critique," she heard him say. Always making jokes.

She continued walking, past the Boston ferns, past the wicker settees, past the romantic illusions, past the hope into the awareness that her own reality was the only true one. She walked into the knowledge that the dreams we hold recede before us no matter what we do to maintain them. But to hold on to dreams is not to cling: Perhaps Walter had misunderstood.

꧁꧁꧁

That was it, of course. One did not dump an entire pitcher of water over the head of an ex-lover, with a goodly portion of it landing on Norman Mailer, and expect to maintain warm personal relations with the man, especially when the act was perpetrated in front of his colleagues, as well as a room full of writer hopefuls, who, Effie suspected, would subsequently look upon Walter Rabinowitz and his cronies with a more jaundiced eye.

Well, so what? Although she had not planned the act, she was not sorry she had done it, for she had thrown one last cold dose of reality on the illusions maintained: hers as well as his. Walter's capacity to delude her had been exceeded only by his capacity to delude himself. But she too had been guilty, as all who deal in sleight of hand, in wordplay, are guilty.

Where fantasy ends, fiction begins.

ॐ ॐ ॐ

Words are a deceit. It didn't happen that way at all, he would say. You give him that. The only reality you hope to transform is your own.

Sometimes—not so often now—you wake in the night and hear his laugh: deep, resonant. The sting behind your cheekbones is the blunt edge of sadness. You try not to think about that. You concentrate instead on the certain way the moonlight catches on the sycamore outside your window. You concentrate on the acrid smell of chaparral just before rain. At this vortex, this still point, you wait in shadow, the longing unquenched by this briefest glimpse into the unfathomable recesses of your freeze-dried heart.

Epilogue

Spring, 1989

The writing group met at Lucy's, which made it easier for her now that baby Jake had arrived. If he was awake, each woman held him in turn, adoring this sweet newcomer in their midst. Lucy was obviously enamored of her son, as were all the women.

"I can't believe my kids were ever that small," Effie said, admiring the baby. "They grow up too fast."

Blythe nodded. "Before you know it, he'll be walking."

Ramona smiled at her niece. "Found any time to write, Lucy?"

"Are you kidding? When he's sleeping, I sleep. I hope in a few months to get back to it, though."

"You will," Effie said. "Just enjoy this time with him. My guess is that Jake is going to be the source of a story or two."

"Funny you said that, Effie, as I do have a few ideas jotted down."

"You see? You don't have to travel far for inspiration." Effie smiled at the young mother, recalling earlier days with her own firstborn.

"Let's get to the stories, shall we?" Ramona said.

Both Blythe and Effie nodded.

"By the way, I loved all of your work this go round."Why don't we look at Effie's story? We haven't heard from her in a time."

"As you no doubt noticed, this piece is very different from my earlier stories. It's a fairy tale of sorts."

"I saw." Blythe encouraged Effie, then all of the women studied the manuscript before them.

A Woman's Cautionary Tale

In times now gone, when it was still of some use to wish for the thing one desired, there lived on a lonely mountaintop a woman who, feeling no longer needed, forsook her home, her grown children, and her worldly possessions to follow her heart, in order to journey toward the emergence of her feminine spirit.

It so happened that one day a silver-tongued Prince was walking through the forest and when he emerged from the woods he saw the woman. When he got nearer to her he spoke, "I have been wandering a lifetime, searching for the answer to my heart's longing. I would like to rest." The woman led him into her house and he was kindly received and hospitably treated. Before long he was enamored of the gentle woman and he thought of nothing else and cared for nothing but pleasing her.

The woman said to him, for she was possessed of magic, "I can see that you carry within you a wonderful treasure. You have the heart of a bird." She looked sadly out her window toward a distant range of hills.

"Why are you so sad?" the Prince asked.

"Dear Prince," was her answer. "I long for what is unattainable."

"And what is that?"

"True love."

"If that is all your trouble," said the Prince, "I can soon lift that burden from your heart." Then he drew her to him and for a time they sat together on the mountain. She listened as he spoke of faraway lands, listened to words pure as honey that flowed from his gilded tongue, listened to poetry as pristine as the song of the meadowlark.

His words were rhapsodies to her ears and he taught her to discourse in like melodies. At last the poet Prince she had expected all her life had come to her.

Soon the Prince grew weary and he lay his head on her lap. She watched him as he slept and longed to know the mystery of his songbird's heart.

For a time the two were very happy. Their spirits soared as one. Because of his love, the woman was able to grow wings of her own and join the Prince in flight. But like the bird whose heart he possessed, the Prince was unable to stay very long in one place. The fiery demon he fought was fear of venturing forth toward the full expression of his heart's vision.

"I cannot stay with you," he told the woman of the mountain, "For I have another life in the world below. I must return there. I have a wife."

"Oh, what treachery is in the world!" exclaimed the woman, and she sank down in her grief. She did not know what to do. She saw that her beloved had betrayed her and once again she was alone on the mountain. She felt very sad and she went into the meadow and cried. Her tears turned to clouds that hid the mountaintop from view. The woman had hoped that the Prince would rescue her from sorrow, but it was not to be.

Bitterness grew within her. She was very angry and hurt and she used her magic powers to fool the man with the raven's heart, as the man had fooled her with the magic of his words.

As the Prince made his way down the cloud-covered mountain to the valley below, he came upon a walled garden. He peeked over the wall and saw growing there beautiful flowers and herbs and fruits. "I am so hungry," he said aloud, and climbed over the wall and picked an apple. He began to eat the fruit. He had barely swallowed one bit when he began to feel very odd and quite changed. He felt his head grow large and from it two long ears emerged. Four furry legs grew as well. To his horror he saw that he had been changed into a donkey.

With his long ears he heard from the far-off mountaintop the trembling voice of the woman who loved him.

He heard her say, "With his words the Prince cast a spell over me. I was forced to forget everything but him. But heaven in a happy hour has taken away my blindness. Now I am really free. All has been a dream. All is illusion."

But the woman's sympathetic heart still stirred with love for the man with the bird's heart so she returned the Prince to his former self, allowing only that the world should remember this sad tale.

That is why today when you see a mist-covered mountaintop, you remember the woman of the hills and know that the clouds are really her tears. And that is why today when you meet a silver-tongued Prince, you are wise to remember that words are easy; it is by deed alone that we distinguish the Prince from the ass.

The women sat quietly. For a moment no one spoke. And then Lucy, young Lucy with babe in arms, said to Effie, "I think you've done it, gal. You've written a fairy tale for vulnerable women, a tale that might have saved you a lot of heartache had you written months ago."

"But writing it did save me," Effie said, acknowledging her friend's words. "Only it saved me after the fact. As all of you have saved me. Thank you so much for being my friends, for standing by me when I was behaving poorly. For listening."

Ramona stood, went over to Effie and gave her a hug. "And what is the woman of the mountaintop going to do now?

"Yes," Blythe said. "What's next?"

"For starters, I'm thinking of trying to find a larger place, one where the girls can have a bedroom of their own." Effie studied her writing group friends, looked at them one by one, noting each precious face.

Then she laughed, a sweet confidant sound the group had not heard from her in a long time. "And, I'm going to write, ladies. I'm going to write."

 **Judie Rae** holds a Master's Degree in Professional Writing. She is the author of four books for young people, including a Nancy Drew Mystery. She also authored a college thematic reader, *Rites of Passage,* and a poetry chapbook *The Weight of Roses*, published by Finishing Line Press. Forthcoming is a second chapbook. *Howling Down the Moon*, from Finishing Line. Her essays have appeared in *The Sacramento* Bee, as well as on San Francisco's NPR station KQED. She has also written for *Outside California, Tahoe Quarterly,* and *Sacramento Magazine,* and online for *Women's Voices for Change.* After twenty-seven years of teaching college English, Judie now concentrates on writing articles and essays primarily related to life in the Sierra Foothills where she lives with her husband, sculptor Will Connell.

Previous Publications

Prescription for Love, A Caprice Romance, 1984. Tempo
     Books
Third Time Lucky, A Caprice Romance, 1984. Tempo Books
Boyfriend Blues, published by Dell, 1983
The Clue in the Camera, a Nancy Drew Mystery, 1988,
     Minstrel Books published by Pocket Books
Rites of Passage: A College Thematic Reader, 2002, published
     by Heinle & Heinle, a division of Thomson Learning

website: www.judierae.com

ADDITIONAL TITLES FROM ARTEMIS BOOKS

Interrupted Lives: Four Women's Stories of
Internment During World War II in the Philippines
by Margaret Sams, Jane Wills, Sascha Jean Jansen, Karen
Kerns Lewis
Edited by Lily Nova and Iven Lourie

ISBN: 978-0-9645181-9-3
$11.95 retail
Edited by
Lily Nova and Iven Lourie

First person memoirs of internment in Santo Tomas prisoner of war camp, Manila, during World War II—a valuable contribution to Women's History and Narratives of Captivity.

Return to Mykonos: Poems by Iven Lourie

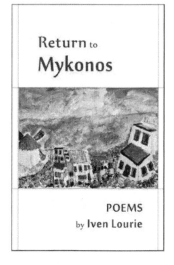

ISBN: 978-0-9645181-7-9
$9.95 retail
(4 watercolor illustrations in color)

A poet's journal of six months traveling in Greece in 1972 during the rule of a military junta plus a series written on return to a liberated Greece in 1998: a mélange of landscape, history, dreams, and sensory details of being in legendary places.

Warlock Rhymer:
An English Translation of Robert Burns' Scots Poems
by Andrew Calhoun

ISBN: 978-0-9645181-4-8
$ 24.95 retail
The first complete translation of
Burns' poems from Scots dialect

"Andrew Calhoun's research is impressive. Not only is he a first-rate Burns' scholar, he also seems to know what Burns felt in his heart…."

—June Skinner Sawyers, author of *Bearing the People Away: The Portable Highland Clearances Companion*

New Life Through Energy Healing:
The Atlas of Psychosomatic Energetics
by Dr. Reimar Banis, M.D.

ISBN: 978-0-9645181-1-7
$49.95 retail, hardcover,
full color printing

A detailed overview of the modalities of energy medicine—useful both for the lay reader seeking self-healing and for the health professional working with energetic and vibrational techniques or any related healing practices.

Delos the Island of Miracles

by Dimitra Voulgaris, George Voulgaris, and. Michael Samuels, M.D.

ISBN: 978-0-9645181-3-1
$19.95 retail
(filled with photos and drawings)

"Much more than an ordinary travel guide, this marvelous book is a portal transporting the reader across millennia to a magical place imprinted on the very DNA of the planet..."
--Dr. Gerald Porter, Provost, Fielding Graduate University

PUBLISHER CONTACT INFO:

Iven Lourie, Editor
Artemis Books
P.O. Box 1108
Penn Valley, CA 95946
USA

cell phone: (530) 277-5380
email: artemisbooks@gmail.com

Comments on *The Haunting of Walter Rabinowitz*:

"Judie Rae writes the internal landscape of the heart with keen insight and empathy. This is the story of the confusion that often comes with love and the will to forge through it and come out the other side."

—Betsy Graziani Fasbinder, author of *Fire & Water: A Suspense-filled Story of Art, Love, Passion, and Madness & Filling Her Shoes: A Memoir of an Inherited Family*

"The narrative pace is quick…. But these main characters' inner struggles to live original lives are related to wider political / social events and currents of thought. In this sense the novel is a novel of ideas as well as one of *becoming*."

—Gene Berson, author of *Raveling Travel*, long-time California teacher and Poet in the Schools.

"Set in the creative writing world of '80s L.A. amid divorce, back-to-the-land garden plots, therapy, and the bonds of women's friendships, Judie Rae's tart and funny twist on the familiar interaction between charming male professors and adoring female students will make you laugh, groan, and perhaps reconsider your own potential for exacting revenge. (Extra credit for picking up the literary references.) Rae's protagonist Effie braids the strands of inner and outer dialogue with writing into a rope connecting her to new strength and understanding. This is one woman's determined venture toward being more fully herself."

--Molly Fisk, First Poet Laureate of Nevada County, CA, and author of *The More Difficult Beauty* (poetry) and several essay collections, most recently *Naming Your Teeth: Even More Observations from a Working Poet*